Praise for
The Thing in the Snow

"Eerily compelling."

—*New York Times*

"Imagine *Severance* alley-ooped to John Carpenter, only to be stolen by Kurt Vonnegut for a dunk on the other end. A subtle comedic powerhouse of claustrophobia and frigid workplace bureaucracy."

—Stephen Markley, nationally bestselling author of *Ohio*

"The absurdity of the modern workplace has inspired copious satires, and like the creators of *Office Space* and *Severance*, Adams winningly skewers corporate life."

—*Washington Post*

"[*The Thing in the Snow* is] in direct line of descent from Heller's *Catch-22*. . . . A quintessential fantastical examination and dissection of the postmodern 'bullshit jobs' ecosystem."

—*Locus*

"A soaring conflagration of absurdity, mystery, and wry humor. This story reads like a Beckett play, in a *Black Mirror* episode, with all the parts played by comedians. A compelling, imaginative, worrying, and hilarious commentary on purpose, priorities, and leadership. Perfect for anyone who has ever questioned why we let time pass and occupy ourselves with busywork ~~~~ ~e things of concern to face."

~~ily Austin, author of *Everyone in This Room Will Someday Be Dead*

"Adams's quirky look at a confined and isolated workspace also offers an almost Stoppard-like look into character development while making a rather bleak but humorous statement about contemporary working life. Though the world Adams created is spare, the reading mind fills every corner with all that is dreamed and feared."

—*Booklist*

"*The Thing in the Snow* is mesmerizing, unnerving, and borderline miraculous. With a novel that's at once cozy and unsettling, Adams has composed a lucid anthem for both the brain-fogged and those whose perception is all too clear. . . . I couldn't stop thinking about it until I finished it—I haven't stopped thinking about it afterward, either, but now I'm not so sure that I want to."

—Calvin Kasulke, author of *Several People Are Typing*

"The strange blend of satire, mystery, and psychological thrills make for a winning combination."

—*Publishers Weekly*

"Who knew there was so much wit in hell? *The Thing in the Snow* is a mystery, an office satire, and a slow-boil study of madness. Trust nothing in this book save for its deadpan brilliance."

—Ryan Chapman, author of *Riots I Have Known*

"Adams succeeds at building tension while exploring the lengths to which people will go to retain power, the narcissism often embodied by those in leadership positions, and the effect of monotony on a person's memory. Inexplicable phenomena can be devastating to the mind, but as this perceptive novel and any undervalued employee can attest, tedium is just as destructive."

—*BookPage*

"Sean Adams does a masterful job balancing wry humor, a mind-boggling mystery, fantastic character work, and a major creep factor. This is my favorite kind of book: a story of big ideas that demands to be finished and sticks with you after you're done."

—Rob Hart, author of *The Paradox Hotel*

"This brilliantly written book will have even the reader questioning everything they think they know about the story as it unfolds."

—*Free Lance-Star*

"Adams lures readers into a world as claustrophobic as a snow globe, then shakes things up with a flurry of satirical commentary on the surreal and absurd nature of workplace culture. . . . A uniquely hilarious yet frightening vision."

—*Little Village*

THE
THING
IN THE
SNOW

ALSO BY SEAN ADAMS

The Heap

THE
THING
IN THE
SNOW

A NOVEL

Sean Adams

wm

WILLIAM MORROW
An Imprint of HarperCollins*Publishers*

HarperCollins books may be purchased for educational, business, or sales promotional use. For information, please email the Special Markets Department at SPsales@harpercollins.com.

A hardcover edition of this book was published in 2023 by William Morrow, an imprint of HarperCollins Publishers.

FIRST WILLIAM MORROW PAPERBACK EDITION PUBLISHED 2024.

Title page art courtesy of Shutterstock, Inc. / Olya Detry

Library of Congress Cataloging-in-Publication Data has been applied for.

ISBN 978-0-06-325776-4

23 24 25 26 27 LBC 5 4 3 2 1

For Muriel

THE
THING
IN THE
SNOW

1.

There are only two others on the caretaking team I supervise: Gibbs and Cline, each I'd estimate about ten years my junior. The thing we take care of is a sprawling building called the Northern Institute, located in a remote region where the snow never melts. I cannot say exactly where. I fell asleep just ten minutes into the helicopter trip here several months ago, and when I awoke shortly before our arrival, all I could see was an endless expanse of white. The Northern Institute had, for a long time, been a lively research facility. Now, having been stripped of its research budget, it is merely a facility. When research halted and the researchers were evacuated, Kay crunched the numbers and deemed it cheaper to hire a small team to look after things than to make the anticipated repairs were the building simply left vacant until research could resume.

And so here we are, the three of us, in my office, drinking coffee, preparing for Friday's work. Outside, a harsh gust howls across the snow's surface.

"Windy out there," I say. "Even worse last night."

Cline does not respond, but instead looks out the window.

"I come from a windy place," Gibbs says, "so I'm fairly used to wind. But yes, it was very windy."

I leave a moment for Cline to contribute to the conversation, but he continues gazing out the window, his eyes thinning to a squint.

"It was whipping so intensely against the walls," I say to Gibbs, "I barely got to sleep."

Gibbs's grip on her coffee mug tightens just slightly. "If you're too tired, and need the rest, I'd be happy to oversee things. For the day, at least."

"That won't be necessary," I say. "I'm not tired."

"But you said you barely slept."

"I said I barely *got to* sleep," I say. "Once I did, I slept quite well." Which is not true. I slept terribly, but I will not admit as much, definitely not to Gibbs.

Something to know: It is not required that I, as supervisor, make my office available for coffee and light socialization each weekday morning before work begins. This I do of my own volition, in the spirit of generosity. But Gibbs and Cline don't seem to realize this. Perhaps, if I'd wanted recognition, I should not have opened my office for coffee and light socialization on our first day here. Perhaps I should've waited a week or two and then said, "Hey, how about I open my office each morning for some coffee and light socialization?" Or maybe just "Hey, how about I open my office each morning for some coffee?" as the outright mention of light socialization might create an atmosphere that is neither light nor particularly social. At any rate, whether I made overt my desire for there to be light socialization is immaterial. The point is, had I waited, the other two might have known a world without coffee and light socialization to look forward to each morning, and then they might see my commitment to going above and beyond and appreciate me more. But I do not feel appreciated. I feel taken for granted and often disrespected, and also powerless to correct matters, as voicing one's desire to be respected and not to be taken for granted is much like voicing one's desire for light socialization—antithetical to achieving the stated goal.

This is the burden under which I must supervise, a burden I am sure Gibbs could not handle, though she thinks she could. She has never stated as much, only inquired about potential for advancement, but given that our ranks here are two-tiered—there is me, the supervisor, and them, the supervised—I understand the subtext. That is why, the few days that Cline could not come down to work—claiming, each time, to be suffering from discomfort in an area of his body he'd prefer not to discuss, an amazingly simple and yet airtight excuse—leaving just Gibbs and me to the task at hand, I made a point to supervise her more vociferously.

Lest I be accused of playing favorites, I also supervised Cline more vociferously when an unnamed feminine issue (another strikingly simple yet foolproof out) caused Gibbs to spend three workdays in her quarters. This, however, is not due to some perceived threat. No, Cline simply requires more vociferous supervision, as Cline is easily distracted, unintelligent, and requires extra motivation just to meet base levels of productivity. And yet, despite these shortcomings, it is Cline and not either supervisor—the current (me) or the hopeful (Gibbs)—who first sees the thing in the snow. Or perhaps it is not strange at all that Cline would be drawn to the window, away from the light socialization, which, light as it may be, and voluntary, is work of a sort.

"Hey," he says, motioning with his mug, "is there something out there? In the snow?"

Gibbs and I discontinue our conversation, each of us grateful for its end, and step over to stand on either side of Cline. The landscape outside is entirely white. A rolling line is the only horizon, separating the white of the snow from the gray of the clouds that forever stifle the sun. But Cline is right. Out beyond the window, something dark glints in the little light that makes it through. There is a thing in the snow.

2.

Our task for the week has been opening and closing the doors.

Kay has asked that we open and close all doors and note if there are any whose mechanisms produce a volume that exceeds "what one would expect." A loud knob or hinge might indicate necessary repairs or replacements that will be added to our task list in the upcoming weeks, once the necessary tools and parts can be gathered and sent our way. We might finish quicker with a divide-and-conquer approach, but Kay made it clear during our onboarding that all tasks are to be completed as a group. I appreciate this, as it allows me to more actively supervise, and ensures a more thorough assessment, since each of us likely has a different idea of what constitutes appropriate door volume. So far, our committee has found no problematically loud doors, although a few have inspired some interesting discussions regarding what constitutes a "creak."

We pick up where we left off the day before, on the fifth floor.

"How did that one sound?" I ask.

"It sounded good to me," Cline says. "Like a door sounds. I didn't hear anything wrong with it. And I was trying to."

I give Cline an approving nod, pleased with how much he's taken to heart my lecture from earlier this week on the difference between not hearing and not listening.

"Gibbs?" I say.

"I'm sorry, I was distracted," Gibbs says.

"It's okay," I say, "let me open it again."

"By the thing in the snow," Gibbs says, before I can put hand to knob.

"We really need to be focusing on the doors here, if we want to finish in time for me to fill out the paperwork," I say.

"I could fill it out," Gibbs says.

"It's not about the paperwork," I say. "It's the part with the doors that takes time."

"Fine," she says.

I open the door again, and Gibbs says it sounds good to her. So we are in agreement: this door is okay.

We move on to the next door, but on our way there, Cline says, "What about now?"

"What about now?" I repeat.

"We could talk about the thing in the snow between doors."

And he's right. It's possible and even a good idea, one I wish I had suggested. But I fear that this could backfire, as I sense the others are excited about this new development, and there is only so much time between doors. Still, I agree.

"Okay, so here's what I'm thinking," Gibbs says. "You know how, this morning, I was telling you about the wind?"

"We were talking about the wind, yes," I say.

"Well, as I said, I grew up in a windy place," Gibbs goes on. "We're talking very strong wind. Wind that could blow out a candle through a closed window."

"Wouldn't that be an issue with the window?" I say.

"What?" Gibbs says.

"If the wind blows through a window," I say, "extinguishing a candle, wouldn't that more likely be evidence of a window's weakness than a wind's strength?"

"It's just a figure of speech," Gibbs says.

"Oh," I say.

"I've heard it," Cline says, almost certainly lying.

"The point is, I grew up in a windy area," Gibbs says. "So I'm well acquainted with the effects of the wind. And I don't think it's a coincidence that we saw the thing in the snow after a windy night."

"Are you saying that the wind carried the thing in the snow, whatever it is, here?"

"That's a possibility," Gibbs says. "But then again, it was still windy this morning, when Cline saw the thing in the snow."

"I noticed that," Cline interjects. "That's why I was looking out the window. I was thinking, 'Wow, it's windy out there.' Windy enough to blow a candle out through a closed window, some would even say. I don't mean these windows." Cline looks at me as he says this. "These windows are very well constructed. Anyway, I was looking out, thinking, 'I wonder if this wind had any effect on the landscape,' something naturally of interest to a painter like me. Landscapes, I mean. Not wind. It's hard to paint wind, unless there are leaves around. Anyway, so I was looking, and then I was like, 'Whoa, what's that thing? In the snow?' It being an interruption of the landscape that I've come to expect, one that I'd like to paint, crazy as it might seem, you know, being just a bunch of white, et cetera. But maybe I could find a way to do it."

"Would you like me to request some painting supplies," I say, "when I fill out the paperwork for Kay this week?"

"No," Cline says. "Not yet."

"Getting back to the thing in the snow," Gibbs says, "what I was saying is that, if it was windy this morning, and the thing in the snow clearly didn't move, then maybe it didn't blow in. Maybe it was uncovered. And the thing in the snow is actually the tip of something bigger."

It is at this point that I realize my fears have come true. We have been standing in front of the next door for I don't know how long. Without addressing Gibbs's assertion—which, I will admit, checks out, and furthermore leaves me unsettled—I open the door and close it.

"Sounded like door noises to me," Cline says.

"Same," Gibbs says.

"Agreed," I say. Another successfully assessed door of appropriate volume.

"So what should we do about it?" Gibbs says.

"The door?" I ask. "We don't have to do anything with the doors that don't make any concerning noises."

"I meant the thing in the snow," Gibbs says. "What should we do about it?"

The truth is, I don't know. The obvious course of action

would be to hike out and see for ourselves, but this is not possible. It's too cold, and besides, we're not permitted out on the snow. It has to do with the strange "snow sickness" the researchers often felt when they lowered themselves out of the third-story windows, even to do something so simple as smoke a cigarette. Some experienced mild light-headedness. Others were overtaken by a severe sense of disorientation that seemed to last a day for every half hour they spent on the frozen surface. Given the limited nature of our positions—as well as the circumstances that led to the research's sudden halt, the nature of which Kay did not elucidate, not even in our one-on-one supervisorial training—it was deemed best to mark the out-of-doors off-limits, excluding the short trips onto the roof for loading and unloading.

Up ahead, the hallway intersects with another, and through the convergence passes a shadow. Cline stops. "Did anyone else see that?"

"It was just Gilroy," I tell him. Then I call his name—"Gilroy!"—but of course he does not resurface or respond.

"Maybe he knows about the thing in the snow," Gibbs offers.

"You can ask him," I tell her. "Cline and I can handle the doors for a minute."

It's an offer I make only because I know she'll decline, and when she does, I have to fight to keep from smiling.

"When we finish up, I'll talk to him," I say.

3.

The others' distaste for Gilroy is not unfounded. Condescending, pretentious, and often outright batty, he's the kind of person who eschews empathy with such vigor that distaste is not just warranted, it is the correct evolutionary response, and anyone who might express a response otherwise would raise red flags about their own penchant for sociopathy.

Gilroy was here when we arrived. He is the last remaining researcher working at the Northern Institute. What he is researching he will not tell me or any of us directly. Instead, he speaks vaguely about how his work seeks to "predict the future of cold," or "critically reevaluate the cold," or "give name to aspects of the cold heretofore unspeakable." I have no idea what that means, nor can I say how he conducts research, as the Northern Institute has been emptied of all research equipment. There remain chairs and tables but no machines or devices and very few containers of any kind. Gilroy requires no such things, apparently. He roams from room to room with a stack of loose papers and records his findings, whatever they may be.

Gilroy occupies two modes, both off-putting. Either you find him standing hunched over a table, engaged in his writing, in which case, he grows angry if you make any noise at all, let alone ask him even the simplest question, or, worse, you stumble upon him staring off at nothing, his eyes glassy. Like this, he is alarmingly forthcoming with his thoughts, all too willing to talk through the endless cold-obsessed turmoil that is his mind. Today, after we're finished with the doors, Cline, Gibbs, and I find him in a room on the fifth floor and discover that he's in the latter state. The other two wait outside as I make my approach.

"Gilroy," I say, "we were wondering if you might be able to help us out. There's something we've noticed, in the snow."

"Something in the snow?" Gilroy says, his tone more attentive than I've heard before. "A person?"

"No," I say. "An object."

Just as quickly, Gilroy's attention goes slack and returns to some far-off place. "Oh," he says.

"And we thought you might know what it is," I say, "seeing as you've been here so long."

"No time for that," Gilroy says. His hands are drawn close together. In his right, he holds a pen, which he taps absentmindedly on his left thumb. I recognize it as the same kind I keep in my desk, the supply of which seems to be forever depleting, but I do not mention this.

"All you'd need to do is look out a window," I say.

"I'm in the middle of something," Gilroy says. "A conundrum."

"Well, I'm sorry to interrupt. I'll let you get—"

But Gilroy cuts me off. "I thought it was snowing, so I went onto the roof in just my sweater and pants, but it was just some of the existing snow, blowing in the wind. At any rate, being out there, it seemed like a good idea to do a little exercise. For my research. So I stood very still until the coldness overtook me."

"I was told by Kay not to go on the roof," I say, "except when depositing files in the lockbox or unloading the tools and the provisions from the hutches."

Gilroy waves his pen in a gesture of dismissal. "It's a clearance-levels thing. What I was saying was, I stood there until the coldness overtook me, which this morning was quicker than usual, with the wind."

"We were talking about the wind," I say, "this morning, when we saw the thing in the snow."

"But I'm not talking about the wind," Gilroy says. "The wind is merely a vessel for the cold. It overtook me with greater ease than normal due to the wind, but it would've overtaken me regardless, no accomplices necessary."

"All right," I say. "Sure."

"So I stood there until I was fully debilitated," Gilroy goes on, "until I truly felt the cold's power, at which point the mere steps it would take to return through the door back to the safety of the Institute's limited comforts seemed like an insurmountable distance. And in this state, when I did not merely feel cold, but rather, when I was one with the cold—when I was perhaps more cold than man, you might say—I sought to write an account of my thoughts. But I couldn't retrieve the notepad from my pocket. I couldn't even grip my pen, for that matter. In fact, I dropped it, and it disappeared into the dusting of snow the wind had blown onto the roof."

I point to the pen in his hand. "Looks like you found it, though."

"This is a different pen," Gilroy says. "The other pen is still out there. Or more likely, it blew away. Another victim of the cold. Just as I would have been, had I not managed to stumble back inside and regain a base level of functionality. Now I stand here, successfully holding this pen." Gilroy holds out his pen in front of him. "And I am trying to put into words what it was like when I, mere hours ago, could not grip a pen. Only, any words I put to paper now will feel disingenuous, as they will be put to paper with a pen that I can not only hold, but also operate with great dexterity."

"You could just do your best," I say, hoping this will relieve him of whatever mental burden compels him to keep talking. Its effect is the opposite.

"It's not a matter of effort," Gilroy responds, adjusting his grip on the pen to a tight, angry squeeze. "It's not a matter of trying to remember what it felt like to lose the ability to hold a pen. That would be like trying to tap into the memory of a stranger. I am not the man who lost the grip of his pen, now that I can hold a pen again, and I wasn't that man in the moments leading up to when I dropped the pen. The second before the pen slipped from my fingers, I was myself. Then, as my grip relinquished, I turned into someone else. That's what the cold does to us. That's why we struggle to understand it. Because we are not ourselves when we are cold. The cold turns us all to imbeciles."

"Imbeciles," I say.

"Yes, imbeciles," Gilroy goes on. "Think about it. The man

who cannot express his thoughts? He might not be intelligent, but he can still be put to use. But a man who cannot even hold a pen? Cannot even reach for his notepad? For whom placing foot before foot in ambulation is a great struggle? What use does he have to the village?"

"What village?" I say.

"The village of humanity," Gilroy says.

The wind no longer whips, so that when Gilroy stops talking, a silence falls over us, one not even interrupted by the buzz of the overhead light fixtures. Gilroy has not turned them on, I realize, and over the course of our conversation the mostly invisible sun has begun to set.

"So you won't take a look at the thing we've seen in the snow," I venture.

"No, no," Gilroy says. "Far too busy for that."

I expect him to begin writing, but he doesn't. He simply stares into the dusky darkness of the room.

Outside, Cline and Gibbs wait.

"What did he say?" Gibbs asks.

"He said he wasn't sure," I say, which feels more or less like the truth.

4.

Most nights, I'd go with the others to the sixth floor, where our various living quarters are located. But it's Friday, so I bid Gibbs and Cline a good weekend and return to my office to fill out the week's paperwork. It is usually just one form, often with only one question. This week's form is more detailed than many. It asks for the number of problematically loud doors, and then beneath demands enumeration of the perceived culprits behind said volume: hinges, knobs, etc. The zero I place in the blank next to the initial question discontinues the need to fill in zeroes next to the various door parts, but I do so anyway, out of a desire for thoroughness.

The paperwork I will then deposit in the lockbox on the roof, where it will be picked up by the helicopter that comes each Friday evening to drop off provisions and tasks for the following week. This is how we can communicate with Kay and relay our progress, if the word "progress" can really be applied to something that is essentially without end. For all demands that cannot wait until Friday, there is a button next to the door to the roof. Press it, and it transmits beeps to a radio in Kay's assistant's office. We've all been trained on the number of times to press the button (and how long to hold each press) in order to communicate a number of emergency scenarios.

Then there are the cards Kay gave to me during our one-on-one supervisorial training. At the top of each one is a simple statement:

I, or a member of my team, have/has experienced the following symptoms at levels beyond what feels normal and for reasons I/ they cannot explain:

Below this are checkboxes for things such as dizziness, confusion, loss of control, disorientation, and a general decrease in motor skills. I am to fill out a card and include it with the week's paperwork only when necessary. Their purpose has something to do with the snow sickness, and Kay assured me I shouldn't need them as long as we stay inside. "We are just covering all of our bases," she explained, but I still make sure to remove a card from their hiding place in the desk and read it carefully each week, as it is my job to take these things seriously. The reason I keep them hidden is because Kay also asked that I not tell the others about them, as Gibbs and Cline may experience a psychosomatic reaction and report symptoms they don't truly have. "The cards are only for times when the symptoms are strong and protracted," Kay told me.

If there's something that cannot be communicated by way of the fields provided by the paperwork, the button, or the cards, I can apply a Post-it note. Early on, I did this each week, giving Kay my assessment of the general mood, or expressing thankfulness for the opportunity to serve in a supervisorial capacity. After several weeks, Kay wrote back a Post-it of her own: *Notes not needed.* Since then, I have applied Post-its rarely, despite an at times overwhelming desire to give some update beyond what can be quantified by the paperwork, not to communicate any particular message to Kay, not even to build camaraderie between us as two people entrusted with the oversight of others (Cline and Gibbs for me; me and many others for Kay). No, I often desire to apply a Post-it note because there are times when it feels like the application of a Post-it note is all I can do to reinforce my existence and remind myself that the tasks we are given here are not merely completed (as is noted on the paperwork) but experienced.

Which is all to say—after checking over my shoulder to ensure I can still see the thing in the snow in the dying light of day—a dizzying excitement overtakes me, the hair on my arms and in my beard standing stiff with goose-pimpled anticipation as I open the top drawer of my desk, retrieve the stack of Post-its, and write a message.

Kay—

There appears to be some sort of thing in the snow, a little ways out to the east of the building. Might this have been left behind by the researchers? If so, please let me know what you believe

it to be so that we can do our best, as caretakers, to ensure its
well-being.

    Best,

    Hart

I adhere the note to the page of the week's paperwork, then climb the stairs to the roof, stopping at my quarters to retrieve my cold-weather wear: a parka, snow pants, hat, and gloves.

Usually, to step out, even just for a moment, serves as an essential part of my week. Even bundled up as I am, even when the wind does not blow as it did last night or this morning, the coldness of the outside serves as an eraser, shocking my mind so that, when I step back inside, I no longer think about the week that has just concluded. To put it differently: to finish the paperwork is to finish the workweek, whereas to step in from the cold is to commence the weekend.

Tonight is different. Even after depositing the folder and returning to my quarters, the thrill from writing the Post-it remains as a thin residue over the night. Slowly, it fades, flaring up again only briefly when I perceive the sharp whirling sound of the helicopter's rotor through the building's thick walls. It grows louder, slows, and then eventually picks up again before receding.

It will be a week before Kay sends her response, given the helicopter's schedule. Likely, there will be a simple explanation, and then no more Post-its for some time, if ever again. So while it feels like a slight to the weekend to hold on to an excitement born from work, I decide I will savor the feeling and let it lull me to sleep.

5.

Another weekend at the Northern Institute.

Early on, when we'd reconvene for coffee and light socialization on Mondays, I'd ask Gibbs and Cline how they'd spent their two days off, only to receive confused looks. I thought it had something to do with my being their supervisor. Perhaps they considered even such a polite inquiry to be a betrayal of contracts both figurative and literal, an attempt to control them in the hours over which my position gave me no control at all. Then, in our third or fourth week here, Gibbs turned the question back on me and I could not answer. I had done only minor things, and I had done them alone, lacking the self-consciousness of company that might lock in some detail worthy of recounting. My memory of whatever insignificant events had occurred over the weekend faded not just by Monday, but in the moments immediately following them. If, before bed on Sunday, I tried to re-create a timeline for the previous two days, it would be inaccurate, the moments floating and reshuffling themselves in a variety of orders, all of which would seem plausible but none of which would seem entirely correct.

Time passes slowly and strangely here on days with nothing to do. On weekday evenings, there is exhaustion to contend with. There is the relief of entering one's quarters, a place of one's own. There is the darkness that invites one under the covers and eases one to sleep. On Saturdays and Sundays, when the exhaustion of the week wears off, there is little to put one's energy toward. And so the hours pass in a series of thoughts and actions, none of which hold any true weight.

I spend more time in bed on the weekends than I would admit to the others. The windows here are thick, the walls well insulated, but before our arrival, to minimize spending, Kay performed a series of calculations to find the ideal temperature at which to set the building's central thermostat: a temperature as low as possible, beyond which our circulation would slow to the point of impeding our work. This temperature was then conveyed to the helicopter pilot who transported us here. We were made to wait in the helicopter as he went inside and set it. This way, we would not know where the thermostat is located, and thus would not be tempted to adjust it ourselves.

When I asked Kay about this temperature during our orientation, she only shook her head. "It is best not to know," she said. "We have associations with certain temperatures as cold and others as warm. If I told you, you might feel colder than you truly are."

I accepted this at the time. But now I do feel cold. We all do. We wear bulky sweaters and fleece-lined pants and sometimes knit hats, and while Kay's team got it right—none of us feel a slowing of circulation, or at least not enough to disrupt the workflow—we still feel cold. Not to the level that so fascinates Gilroy, but cold nonetheless. The only truly warm places in all of the Northern Institute are our beds, for which we've been given special blankets. I spend many weekend hours under that blanket, drinking tea or coffee, which I brew using an electric kettle supplied to me. I fill it up to the top in the bathroom down the hall so that I may enjoy three or four cups without having to leave my bed for a refill, lounging about and wasting hours in a way perhaps unbefitting of a man with my level of responsibility, but so be it.

I try my best not to think about work or the others, although they enter my imaginings from time to time. I try my best not to think about anything, really, to picture the entirety of my existence as ending at the door of my quarters. I think of myself as the inhabitant of some tiny craft the size of my room hurtled into space; a specimen, but not one of note—a mere example of humanity.

It is not a pleasant thought, to imagine myself even more detached from civilization than I already am, but that's the point. If I can achieve this, my theory goes, then maybe, come

Monday (whenever it may be), the limited amount of civilization that I have access to will suddenly feel like a great gift, one that will carry me gleefully through the week, even as Cline continues to make the most basic of mistakes and Gibbs constantly attempts to undercut me.

It has yet to work for more than an hour, but I try again and again, hoping for some breakthrough.

When I cannot separate myself from reality by sheer force of will, I turn to books. I'm reading the Leader series, by the author Rodney Stuyvesant Jr. It began many decades ago, which makes for some oddly dated material, but more important, it means I can continue reading them indefinitely, as there is as close to an unlimited supply as you can have with something like that.

They are not leadership books. They are novels about a man named Jack French, who, after a successful career accruing wealth by leading several large businesses to record-breaking gains, retires at the age of thirty-six. He wants nothing more than to find some peace in which to write his masterwork, a definitive guide to management. Only, each attempt to find such peace lands him unwittingly in a dire situation demanding the kind of exceptional leadership only he can provide. For example, in book four (*Engineering Survival*), he takes a room in a small mountain lodge, the rest of which is occupied by a group of sculptors and ceramicists on a retreat. But when a landslide covers the building, he must coach the others, all incapable of seeing beyond their chosen building materials, to combine their various abilities of assemblage toward constructing a materially diverse machine that will allow them to clear the mud away from within.

I've greatly enjoyed every book so far, but I'll admit that I requested them for pragmatic reasons. Provisions are provided for us, but all nonessential items requested are deducted from our weekly pay. Furthermore, the request form must be submitted to Kay with the week's paperwork. Thus, I had to find books that could hit two marks: first, I needed them to be sufficiently inexpensive, which the Leader books are, given their age and mass production; and, second, I desired to read fiction, as that would best distract me from the reality of our situation here. However, I also wanted to show Kay that I take seriously the responsibility bestowed upon me, hence the appeal of a series of thrillers about leadership.

And certainly, there are some lessons to gain from reading them. For example, in book two (*Sailing with Assailants*), when Jack French, having taken a cruise that is hijacked by seafaring terrorists, finds himself encamped with the members of the band, who play soft jazz during the meal hours, he gives each of them a task to regain control of the ship, but conspicuously leaves the saxophonist out. When the saxophonist asks him why, Jack French smiles knowingly because he had intuited correctly that the saxophonist needs to work on being more assertive. (The move pays off in the book's exciting conclusion, in which the saxophonist's reed plays a shocking role.) This could be taken as a lesson in effective leadership, one I do not exactly know how to apply, as a lack of assertiveness is not an issue my small team suffers from.

Still, if I read far enough, perhaps something will come in handy.

When my room begins to feel small, and the blanket, warm as it is, too confining, I get out of the suite for some exercise.

There is no workout room, so we must make the space our gym. I've heard Cline running up and down the stairwells and passed rooms where Gibbs is jumping rope. I prefer walking. As a way of occupying my mind during these jaunts, I try to figure out just how many rooms there are in the Northern Institute. It seems likely that Kay told us during our orientation and I simply forgot, just as I don't remember exactly how many hours by helicopter it is from here back to civilization, or our exact GPS coordinates, or under what country's jurisdiction this area lies.

I have tried many methods for discerning the number of rooms, such as counting how many there are on a given floor and then multiplying it by six and adding one (for the seventh-floor amphitheater). Ultimately, this will be inaccurate. The floors are not laid out identically, with hallways branching off from the main loop at different intervals on each floor, leading to closets and small interior offices.

Another method: I look for the room on the fifth floor with the largest number I can find. Why I stop at the fifth floor is because the residential sixth-floor rooms are classified by suite number and a letter (I live in 5c, for example), and so will have to be manually added to the total. This method is also inaccurate, though. Some rooms are not numbered, such as meeting rooms and special laboratories (or so they seem to have been; it's hard to tell, given they're empty of everything but chairs and tables now). Bathrooms too, which I avoid (the idea of sharing a bathroom space with someone on the weekend gives me great anxiety). Are these rooms included in the count but not given numbers, or do they exist outside the general scheme?

What's more, I have taken many laps of the fifth floor, and each time, I seem to find a room with a higher number than I remember seeing previously. Whether this is a failure of memory or observation, I cannot be sure. All that is certain is that it is a failure of some kind.

Most of the time, I restrict my weekend walks to the first and second floors. Gibbs and Cline avoid them. Even Gilroy rarely ventures so low in the building. This is likely because of the snow; it piles up to just below the third-story windows. Consequently, the first two floors are entirely snowed in, rendering them especially dark and claustrophobic.

Despite the fact that, according to Kay, they had to melt and excavate fifteen feet of snow to lay the foundation, the construction team still put a doorway on the ground floor. I don't know why. Perhaps there's some law that states there must be a door where a building meets the ground. Or perhaps the builders made the decision on their own. Kay did not spend too much time discussing them, except to imply that their involvement had something to do with a "work release program" except "not from a prison, exactly" and that they were prone to unpredictable behavior. When Gibbs asked if any of them had suffered from the snow sickness, Kay said only, "It would be hard to tell." Whatever the reason, they also put another door on the second floor as a backup, but this serves no purpose either, as the snow has covered it too. Aside from the disorientation one apparently feels when walking on the snow's surface, this is another unique feature of the region: it is the only polar area that has seen a consistent decrease in temperature and increase in snow, year over year. There are no seasons here, aside from winter, and even that resembles no winter I have ever experienced.

All of this is to say, the first two floors are entirely lit by overhead lights: the fluorescents in the halls, incandescent fixtures in the various rooms. Down there, you see things you might otherwise never notice. For instance, it was only during my walks through the first and second floors that I realized all of the flooring tile in the entire Institute is a muted mint green. In the natural light upstairs, the color is almost impossible to notice. It seems to accept the limited daylight that streams through the windows, conforming into a color that does not exist, a color neither as eye-catching as a green nor as noticeably drab as a gray; a color that, were it rendered into a crayon, would simply be called "floor" and no one would question why.

Certainly, this is by design. What little I know about Kay is that every decision she makes is in deliberate pursuit of efficiency. Like the temperature, like our list of tasks, like our very being here—Kay does not make decisions based on aesthetics, unless you consider a tidy spreadsheet an aesthetic.

For that reason, I find her both terrifying and inspiring.

I don't find the first two floors as eerie as the others do. Or, I didn't before. I, for one, enjoyed the knowledge of there being nothing beyond the walls but hard-packed snow. It added to the feeling I sought to achieve on the weekends, one of total isolation.

This desire, I should clarify, is not born of some antisocial tendency. I simply like to give myself over to things completely. When I am reading, I do not like to put down the book until it is finished. When I am working, I do not like to be distracted. When I am supervising the others, I want to feel some sense of authority. In this vein, when faced with something as isolating as a weekend in a mostly abandoned research facility, I choose to embrace the solitude rather than try to alleviate it.

In the first several weeks, I thought the best way to do this would be closing all of the doors in the hallways on my walks through the first or second floor. But this had the opposite effect; it gave the impression of some quietly bustling space, as if each room might contain any number of workers completing projects in hectic silence. So I opened the doors again, and from time to time I would flip a light switch in one of the rooms and stare at its windows darkened completely by densely packed frozen snow, telling myself it was the edge of the world.

This weekend, though, I struggle to do so. Try as I might, I

27

cannot shake Gibbs's theory. What if, somewhere beyond these windows, the base of some massive object lingers, its top only recently made visible to us? And though it is an object and not a living thing—we can be sure of nothing except that—the sense of isolation I seek never quite settles in. The windows continue to frame nothing, but when I stare at them, I see not the edge of the world, but a swirling dark mystery containing innumerable secrets.

And then, eventually, it is Sunday evening, the only time in the entire weekend, aside from Friday night, that feels distinct. Despite having drunk much coffee and spent much time resting and reading, my only exercise being a series of laps (which I did perhaps today, or yesterday, or maybe both days), I am tired and ready for sleep. So, I lie down and turn out my light.

In this way, another weekend at the Northern Institute passes.

6.

Just as I exit the week with a blast of cold, so too do I enter it. Each Monday morning, I get up early, dress for the outside, and walk to the roof to unload the provisions and weekly assignments that had been delivered on Friday.

The reason for this delay is threefold. First, the food Kay's team sends is composed of frozen meals prepared precisely to our individual dietary needs (and vaguely to our individual dietary preferences), and they can withstand a few days on the roof without issue. Second, the cold air invigorates me, leaving me chipper and alert to the demands of the new week when I might otherwise be rubbing the crust of the weekend out of my eyes. Most important, it means that I cannot sneak a look at the task for the week ahead and then agonize over it for the entirety of Saturday and Sunday. Instead, we learn our tasks together each morning, as a group. This, like the coffee and light socialization, is a gesture of goodwill that has gone insufficiently recognized.

When the others arrive at my office sometime later, they fill their mugs from the carafe and we form our typical tableau—me standing behind the desk, Gibbs across from me, Cline by the end table with the coffee machine on it—but a different energy occupies the room. Cline's silence seems born of something beyond a wandering mind. If anything, he appears to be focusing so deeply that he cannot speak, as he stares into the corner of the room. Gibbs, meanwhile, feigns a casual glance around, but her eyes lock on the window just a bit too long, giving her away. Just as on Friday, an unending white occupies the entirety of the view, interrupted only by a small black shape, the thing in the snow.

"I was glad the wind died down on Friday," I say. "Before I had to go onto the roof, I mean."

Gibbs has raised her mug to her lips, but lowers it now without drinking, turning to me. "What was that? There's something on the roof?"

"No," I say. "Just commenting on the wind, or lack thereof."

"Oh, right," Gibbs says. "Will there be more wind, do you know?"

"I don't know," I say. "I don't think they do a forecast for up here."

"Ah," says Gibbs.

The office quiets again. I finish my coffee, and move to get a refill. I can see that neither Cline nor Gibbs has taken a sip of theirs.

"Why don't we take these to go," I say. When neither of them responds, I add, "We can bring along some paper towels, for cleaning up any coffee rings we leave behind."

"Wait, sorry," Cline says, suddenly snapping out of whatever reverie he's been lost in. "What are we doing?"

"I'm glad you asked," I say, stepping to my desk, where I've placed the paperwork for the week, positioning myself to block Gibbs's view out the window. I flip the folder open, read the assignment for the week, and report back to the others: "Chairs. This week Kay would like us to test chairs."

"Will we do anything about the thing in the snow?" Gibbs asks.

"What is there to do but look at it?" I say.

At this, Cline shifts his attention to the window and Gibbs bobs just slightly on her heels, trying to see around me.

"I mean there really is nothing we can do about the thing in the snow," I clarify. "So we might as well focus on the chairs. Shall we?"

Cline turns from the window, looking from Gibbs to me. "But we haven't finished our coffee yet."

7.

The assignment's instructions call for us to sit in each chair in the Northern Institute. Once seated, we are to remain that way at least ten seconds and shift our weight ("within reason," the instructions say, "for example, an amount of shifting equivalent to that of someone reaching for something while sitting") to measure the chair's stability.

I decide that we should begin on the first floor and work our way up. We start with a room we call "the Cubicle." This name refers to its size, significantly smaller than many of the others, making it an ideal starting place for most tasks; the quick completion of a room can give us momentum that we might carry into the rest of the week. The chairs here are the same we see everywhere in the Institute: dark blue plastic seat and back support, held by an aluminum structure. Like an extension of the muted green floor, they are built for anonymity.

"Mine's stable," Gibbs says.

"Mine as well," I say. I turn to Cline, who sits still, staring up at the overhead light fixture. "And yours?"

"What?" Cline says.

"Your chair," I say.

Cline looks from the ceiling to his seat, as if surprised to find it underneath him. "It's fine, I guess. Not very comfortable, but what are you going to do?"

"We're not concerned with comfort. Only stability."

"Oh, right, sorry." Cline shifts his weight in a wild way that I would not define as within reason. "Sure, stable."

"Good," I say, and we each move on to another chair.

The paperwork, as usual, gives no hint to the totality of our work, in this case how many chairs there are. I am asked only for the number of chairs requiring replacement. And so I am not prepared for the sheer amount we are expected to assess. They far exceed any reasonable number of chairs a group of researchers might require, with as many as four packed behind desks, and the rest arranged around tables in a way that would leave no room for even the narrowest set of shoulders. And this is not all. There are more, stacked in corners or generally strewn about. I guess I'd never noticed before, as I only ever occupy two chairs here: the one in my office and, more rarely, the one in my quarters.

The chairs, along with the tables and desks, were left behind when the Institute was evacuated of its researchers, as they had been deemed, according to Kay, "furniture ancillary to research." Why the various pieces of research equipment were taken and these lesser pieces left behind I am not entirely sure. Likely, the beakers, microscopes, centrifuges, and other such items I assume were here could be put to use elsewhere, but it also seems to have been a precautionary measure. I distinctly remember Kay saying it was important to their bottom line that, for the time being, the Northern Institute be a place where "research cannot possibly occur." (Surely excepting Gilroy's work.)

The number of chairs on which we must sit does not shock me simply because of the work it will take, though. What I find truly shocking is what the number of chairs implies: the existence of tables that the researchers did not leave behind, tables that were not deemed "furniture ancillary to research," tables whose connection to the research would go beyond simply holding necessary research equipment. Tables into which said equipment might be built, say, or tables whose unique surface might stimulate intellectual discovery. But try as I might, I cannot picture what such a table would be like. This, like the thing in the snow—whose existence went unknown to me these months, and whose function and size remain unclear—fills me with momentary shame. I am the sole authority figure present, and, as such, I should have the answers.

Then again, if I've learned anything from Jack French and the books in the Leader series, it is that you don't need to know everything, as much as you need to know how to empower those you seek to lead by leaning on their strengths and expertise. So if, say, Gibbs knows what a table that is not ancillary to research is, and I do not, my lack of knowledge would not make her a better leader than me, only a person with a broader knowledge of tables, a knowledge that I, as a supervisor, would be smart to find a use for. (For the record, I do not ask Gibbs if she could imagine such a table, one not ancillary to research, as I fear, even if she also cannot, she will lie and say she can.)

These thoughts do not come one after another, rapidly, but gradually over the course of the day, a chain whose links I forge during the ten-second intervals spent sitting and shifting (within reason). We don't speak except to report our current chair's stability. Our progress is steady but slow, and by day's end, we have barely finished the first floor.

As we make our way up the stairs, done for the day, I can't help noticing that the thrill of the thing in the snow's discovery has completely receded, the product, surely, of our working from the ground up, which had been my idea. We could've easily started with the rooms on the same floor as my office (the third) and worked our way up or down, but we didn't. I'd made the decision to begin with the first floor, where the windows looked out onto nothing but the darkness of densely packed snow, and as a result, our day had been productive. This, along with my willingness to admit my lack of knowledge when it comes to research-aligned tables (just not aloud, and definitely not to Gibbs), fills me with a pride in my leadership I have not felt in some time.

Only when we come to the sixth floor and are ready to depart for our respective quarters for the night does Cline say, "Anyone else notice the lights have been weird?"

"No," I say, "can't say I have."

"I haven't been paying attention to them," Gibbs says.

"Oh," Cline says. "Okay."

And with that we go our separate ways. An innocuous exchange, but still I find myself replaying it over and over in my mind throughout the evening. Only much later in the night do I realize what's troubling me: Gibbs did not say yes to Cline's question, but she also didn't say no.

8.

The next morning, after coffee consumed in silence, without even the lightest of light socialization, we proceed to the second floor and begin sitting once again, at which point I realize something is very wrong.

The rooms contain fewer chairs than those on the first floor, yet we are moving noticeably slower. At least, I notice it. Neither Cline nor Gibbs pays attention to anything but the lights. Gibbs feigns an inquisitive pose, as if she has raised her head in thoughtful consideration of her chair's stability. Yet her gaze always just happens to land on the exact point in the ceiling where the light fixture hangs, regardless of the room. This only emboldens Cline, who gawks at it openly. Yesterday, Gibbs issued her report on each chair's stability promptly, and Cline generally followed suit. Today, I find myself calling out each step of the process: first to sit, then to shift, then to report back to me, and finally to move on to another chair. The rigidity leaves me with almost no time for my own thoughts.

Still, the others' fixation on the lights does not explain the full extent of the slowdown, the true root of which reveals itself shortly after lunch, when I observe Cline sit and subsequently shift his weight upon a chair that I'd already checked myself. After this, I begin to pay much closer attention to their progress from chair to chair, and watch in horror as Cline and Gibbs, preoccupied as they are, sit and shift their weight on chairs that have already been sat and shifted upon twice or even three times over. At one point, Cline and Gibbs pay so little attention to the task at hand that they stand from their seats and each drift to the chair the other had just been sitting in, as if switching places in some kind of lethargic game.

I must do something, so as we rise to change seats in only the third room of the afternoon, I turn to Cline.

"Cline," I say, "I can't help but notice your attention remains fixed on the lights. Are you seeing something that you'd like to share with us?"

The tone I hope to strike is that of the teacher who asks the child giggling in the farthest row of desks if he has something to share with the class, thus drawing attention to him and driving him into a fearful silence. It doesn't work.

"Actually, yes," Cline says. He plops down in a chair I am almost certain Gibbs has already sat in, and for a period far exceeding ten seconds he remains this way, not shifting but speaking. "So, since you brought it up last week—painting, I mean, getting some painting supplies—I spent the weekend really thinking, could I paint here? Which essentially boils down to: How's the light? Because at the end of the day, painting is seeing. At least, in most cases. I did a retreat once where we spent a weekend doing self-portraits in the dark. It was supposed to be in a cave, but there was an issue. Something about falling stalactites. Or maybe a rockslide. Anyway, we had to get one of the community rooms at the library with no windows and turn the lights off. Still, a transformative experience. Like, you spend all that time painting, and the product looks nothing like you and also it *is* you, you know?"

"But you were saying, about the light here," I say, rising and moving to a different chair, an attempt to lead by example. The others remain where they are.

"Yes," Cline says. "So, I spent the weekend doing . . . it's just kind of a painter thing, I don't know exactly what you would call it."

"A survey of the light," I offer.

"An assessment of the light," Gibbs counters.

"Right," Cline says, "an assessment of the light. Because, obviously, there are plenty of rooms without windows here, where I could sit around all Saturday and Sunday, just knocking out self-portraits in the dark if that's what I were into. But my thing is, if I'm going to paint here, I'm going to paint *here*, know what I mean?"

"Sure," I say.

"Absolutely," Gibbs says.

"What I mean is, the first time I said 'here' there, I was talking about just being here," Cline says, "but the second time, I was talking about what I'm going to paint."

"Understood," I say.

"I already sat there," Gibbs says.

It takes a moment for me to realize she's talking to me, about the chair over which I stand. And to think, this is my reward for holding my tongue when she and Cline had done the same thing repeatedly, which is to say nothing of the fact that I have at least made an attempt to work during this conversation, while she and Cline have remained in the same seats for the duration. I can feel myself internalizing this moment as it happens, stashing it away to think about later as I struggle to sleep, imagining any number of different outcomes than the one that transpires, which is that I tell Gibbs, "Good catch," and suggest a new system: once we've properly sat upon a chair, we should relocate it to the far wall of the room. The conversation ceases for a moment as we clear the chairs we feel certain have been tested. Gibbs notably does not move the chair she'd been sitting in, a subconscious admission that she had not administered an appropriate amount of shifting to deem that chair assessed.

Once the chairs are sorted, I see that there are still many left un-sat-upon. These we line up in three equal rows. I sit in the final row, Gibbs in the middle, and Cline at the front, and we work our way through them, sitting and shifting until I call out that it's time to switch. It's an efficient solution, one that I might be proud of, but I find any potential satisfaction offset by the continued conversation about the lights.

"So, I went to a room on the fifth floor with large, clean windows," Cline says. "And I thought, were I to put in my request for some painting supplies, this could be my painting room. But there was something off. I couldn't tell what. Not yet."

"Switch," I call, and we move to the next chair.

"So I went to the next room. Same problem. And I still couldn't figure it out, not all weekend. I kept going around from room to room and all of them seemed off."

"Switch," I say, and we switch.

"But then, yesterday, I realized the problem. In each room, I'd turned on the overhead lights, rather than relying solely on the natural light from the windows, since the light outside here is often very weak."

"Switch," I say, and we switch.

"And that was it. It's not the light coming from outside. It's the light fixtures. There's something wrong with them, but I'm not sure what."

"Like they flicker, very faintly," Gibbs says.

"Yes!" Cline turns to Gibbs, and I open my mouth to reprimand him but ultimately fall silent. Motives aside, this constitutes the most reasonable chair-testing shift Cline has performed these past two days.

"I noticed it too," Gibbs says. "After you mentioned it last night."

"Yes!" Cline says.

"Switch," I say, and we switch.

"Almost like there's some sort of disruption," Gibbs says.

"Yes!" Cline says.

"Like a frequency that is playing upon the lights," Gibbs says.

"Yes!" Cline says.

We have reached the ends of our rows, so I motion for us to move on to the next room, but Gibbs does not seem ready to leave just yet.

"And I think I know what it is," she says. "The disruption, I mean. I think it's the thing in the snow."

9.

Gibbs provides no evidence beyond timing to back up this preposterous claim. Cline noticed the disturbance in the light this past weekend, right after the thing in the snow's surfacing; that's all. Cline, for his part, summons little response beyond an astonished "Huh." I want to call out the ridiculousness of this thinking, but the revelation turns out to be a blessing in disguise. Now that the topic has been broached, neither Cline nor Gibbs pays attention to the light fixtures for the rest of the day. And with our new system of lining chairs up and making our way across them, we manage to finish the second floor fifteen minutes before five.

This quiet momentum keeps up for the following two days, and what's more, the chairs reduce with each subsequent floor. As a concession to the others now that we are above snow-level, I line up the chairs facing the windows in rooms on the eastern side of the building so they can view the thing in the snow as they sit and shift their weight. By Thursday, all we have left are the fifth floor, the sixth floor—which should be easy, since this is where the employee quarters are located and each room has only one or two chairs—and the amphitheater on the seventh. After our coffee, we proceed to our first stop, flip the lights on, and find Gilroy standing in the center of the room with his eyes closed. Most of his clothes are strewn across the floor. He wears nothing beyond a ratty undershirt and a pair of boxer briefs.

Cline stares before looking blankly down at his boots. Gibbs turns, feigning interest in the wall behind us. I shield my eyes. "Sorry," I say. "We can move to a different—"

"No, it's fine," Gilroy says. "I was just finishing up." I can hear him moving around, gathering his things. He does not seem to be in a rush. "It's strange, you know? You try to get in touch with the cold by stripping all of your man-made protections, but is that even *true* cold? I mean, if there is apparel with which to combat it readily available? It's impossible to totally access your cold self that way. Your body never fully gives itself over, knowing that there's a sweater there, easily within reach. True cold, that of which I am forever in pursuit, cares not for your sweater. It makes obsolete even the most advanced synthetic materials churned out by the quote-unquote warmth industry. All of my work, it all blindly gropes at the outer edge of that kind of cold."

I venture a glance over my hand and am relieved to see Gilroy fully dressed. Gibbs and Cline follow suit and the four of us stand there, waiting for whatever will come next, which I imagine is that Gilroy will wander out—greetings and farewells, as well as most basic social cues, not being a strength of his—leaving us to our work.

Instead, he asks, "Have any of you ever experienced a cold like that?"

Gilroy speaks the words quietly, his tone that of a man trying to hide the desperation of asking us, a group of lowly custodians, for help.

"No," I say.

"I don't believe so," Gibbs says.

"Wait, are we talking about cold like temperature, or *a* cold, like getting sick?" Cline says.

"Hmm," Gilroy says.

"Should we line up the chairs?" Gibbs asks the question a little too forcefully. She would like this conversation to be over.

"Chairs," Gilroy says, his eyes settling on me.

Perhaps I should feel flattered. Not only does he show some basic understanding of our hierarchy, this is the most Gilroy has ever tried to engage with us as anything other than three mobile objects that occasionally disrupt his work. But I do not feel flattered. I feel suddenly embarrassed. The efficiency with which we've arranged the chairs, sat upon the chairs, and shifted our weight upon the chairs—a system of which, moments ago, I'd felt exceedingly proud—suddenly seems so stupid, so trivial. Each week, Kay sends a formal description of our assignment and paperwork that must be filled out to authenticate its completion. These tasks feel crucial, because all involved—Kay and her team, me and my team—treat them as such. But Gilroy is not a part of that system, and his continued presence recasts everything. They're just chairs, and we're just sitting in them. That is my job this week: I sit, professionally. How can I express such a thing to someone like Gilroy, a man devoted to thinking, something that inhabits a vastly different stratum than sitting?

"We're doing a series of tests," I say, "to ensure the structural integrity of the chairs."

Gilroy considers this. "Huh," he says.

"Any complaints?" Gibbs asks.

"What?" Gilroy says.

"About the chairs," Gibbs says. "Any complaints?"

Gilroy looks around the room, as if noticing them for the first time. "Oh. None from me. But I don't use chairs. Have not for some time."

"Not even when you're writing?" Gibbs says.

Gilroy shakes his head. "No."

"Doesn't it hurt your back?" Cline asks.

"I don't like to get comfortable when I collect my thoughts," Gilroy says. "I find that when I do, the comfort drives me to collect more thoughts than are necessary. Thoughts that only serve to prolong my state of comfort and, in turn, distract me from my work."

"Oh," Cline says.

"Well, we better get to it," I say, nodding to Gibbs. She and Cline go about collecting the chairs and lining them up in the center of the room.

Gilroy watches them a moment, and then heads for the door. I follow him out into the hall, my curiosity from earlier this week overriding my sense of humility. "Gilroy," I call after him, softly.

He stops and turns around quickly. "What is it? Have they sent you a forecast? Is snow expected?"

"They don't do a forecast for up here," I say for the second time this week.

"Oh, right," he says. "That's the real problem with this place, isn't it? No forecast."

"Sure," I say, but only to move things forward. Truthfully, the lack of forecast would not rank within my top ten inconveniences of life in the Northern Institute. "Anyway, there's something I wanted to ask you."

"Is this about looking out the window again?" Gilroy says.

"No, it's something else."

"It doesn't matter. Whatever it is, I'm too busy."

"But we were just talking," I say.

He sighs. "Exactly. That's what being busy is. It's a compaction. I wasn't busy before because I had enough time to complete the things I have left to do today. Then I spoke to you, which took time, which means I will have to compact the remaining work into less time than I had slotted for it. Hence, I'm busy."

"I just wanted to know," I say, keeping my voice down so the others don't hear, "what were the special tables like? The ones they took out from the first and second floors?"

"Special tables?" Gilroy says, his voice growing somehow sharper. "What have you been reading?"

"I just wanted to know about the special ones," I say. "The ones ancillary to research."

"I don't follow," Gilroy says.

"There are so many chairs and so few tables," I explain. "Some tables must've been taken out due to their close relation to the research being done."

"There are more chairs on the first and second floors," Gilroy says, "because the first and second floors are essentially the basement. With no natural light, few people chose to work there. So if someone working on the third floor or higher needed to remove chairs to make room for something, that's where they took them."

"Oh," I say. "So there are no specialty research tables?"

"No," Gilroy says. "And now I'm even busier." With that, he leaves, making his way briskly down the hall.

I move to return to the room with the others and find Cline coming out the door. "He forgot his stuff," Cline says, holding up a piece of paper.

"Gilroy!" I call. "You forgot your work!"

But he makes no response before disappearing around a corner.

I take the paper from Cline, fold it, and place it into my pocket. "I'll hold on to this. I would hate for Gilroy not to have proof of what he's been up to if there were some sort of audit."

After the short distraction of dealing with him, we make swift progress through the fifth floor, and move on to the empty quarters. These are separated into a series of suites, four rooms around a bathroom. We've spaced ourselves out, so that each of us is the only one in our given suite, allowing us to close the door to the hall and experience unilateral bathroom access. I decide Cline and Gibbs have proven themselves more than capable of the chair work, so I assign them three suites each—their own and two others. I tell them to simply inform me of any chairs requiring replacement when we reconvene in the morning for our coffee, and we go our separate ways.

Not surprisingly, neither of them have any issues to report the next day, nor do I. Something seems to be bothering Cline, though, and when he opens his mouth to speak, I fear he'll bring up the lights again, or the thing in the snow.

"So," he says, "where does Gilroy sleep?"

"What do you mean?" I ask.

"Well, in the suites I checked, there was only my room that was occupied," he says. "Did either of you have his suite?"

"I didn't," Gibbs says, her voice registering some alarm.

"I did," I say, and this relieves the others.

It isn't true, though. None of the rooms in the suites I assigned myself appeared to be occupied, aside from my own. Still, I don't want to unnerve the others with this information, as our run-in with Gilroy yesterday, strange as it began and unpleasantly as it ended, felt like a breakthrough of sorts. I don't know exactly what we stand to gain from better relations with him, aside from a more convivial workplace. But even this seems worth the white lie. After all, there must be some reasonable explanation.

10.

The amphitheater occupies the entirety of the seventh floor, an enormous open room filled with chairs facing a small raised stage. Behind the stage stands a wall constructed entirely of glass that is, Kay told me, nearly two feet thick. And still, the room remains forever colder than the rest of the Northern Institute. It seems like a frivolous design choice, made more frivolous by the fact that it looks out on nothing but the unending white expanse. That is, until last week.

Considering the angle of the room, the obstruction of the stage, and the fact that the floor isn't sloped in any way, it seems impossible that we'd be able to see the thing in the snow from the seats in the audience. But we can. From every single one of them. The others seem to enjoy this, but I do my best to ignore it by glaring at the tight bun of Gibbs's hair, sticking out from under her knit cap.

The chairs, many as there may be, are already arranged in neat rows, and it does not take us long to complete our work. We finish before lunch, which would usually concern me, but this week, the early finish feels like a great victory. We have outdone Kay's expectations. We have been more efficient than even she, a beacon of efficiency, could imagine. This brings me great satisfaction.

And making it all the more satisfying is the contrast between the week's beginning and its end. We started with a stray observation about a disruption of the light, followed by a wild leap of a theory concerning said disruption. But we've ended it quietly going about our work.

I conclude the week just as I end every week: asking Cline and Gibbs if they'd like me to put in an order for anything from Kay.

"A radio," Gibbs says.

"A radio?" I ask. "Why?"

"I'd like to listen to the radio," Gibbs says.

"I could order you a tape player and a book on tape," I say. "Or some music, perhaps. But I assure you, a radio will be useless. There's no signal out here."

"We don't know that for sure," Gibbs says.

"What are you talking about?" I say.

Gibbs doesn't answer, but looks to Cline, who looks at the lights lining the ceiling. We'd turned them on, as the back of the room, farthest from the glass wall, was a bit dim earlier in the morning. Now I wish we hadn't.

I do my best to keep my tone as precise and controlled as possible. "I don't think it's a good idea to embarrass ourselves by requesting a radio from Kay to investigate something to do with the lights that is likely the result of faulty wiring."

"So you see it too," Cline says.

"No," I say. "I was speaking hypothetically. I'm only saying, were there to be some pulsation of the light—which I'm not sure there is—it would likely be the result of wiring, not something buried in the snow suddenly buzzing to life, simply because its tip was revealed by a windstorm, which itself is still nothing more than a supposition."

And I believe this—about the wiring, I mean—though it should be said: I have not noticed anything about the lights because I have ardently avoided looking at the lights since our initial discussion of them. I have even turned off the lights in my quarters early each evening this week to avoid thinking about them, and also to get more sleep (ultimately, a failure).

"And we can't go out there," Gibbs says.

"Correct," I say.

"But that doesn't mean we shouldn't inspect the thing at all, does it?" Gibbs says. "Besides, you wouldn't be embarrassing yourself. If anyone would be embarrassed, it would be me. You just hand in the form."

"Exactly, *I* hand in the form," I say, and this comes out shriller than I would hope. "And there's a reason for that. There's a reason why I fill out the paperwork too. It's because I've been put in charge, and therefore, I am the first line of defense. Kay relies on me to oversee things here, but moreover she relies on me not to waste her time. So, were I to request a radio, even on your behalf, it would reflect poorly on me."

"Okay, but—" Gibbs tries.

"Someone has to get these things, you know," I say. "If we ask for a radio, someone will have to go out and find an appropriately affordable radio. That will be time spent so you can investigate something that is nothing more than an absurd hunch. So no, I won't request a radio."

"You can do that?" Gibbs says, crossing her arms. "You have the authority to simply deny a request? For something I'd spend my own money on?"

I ignore this and turn my attention to Cline. "How about you? Anything to request? Those painting supplies?"

"Another chair," Cline says.

"Another chair?" I'm coming apart completely now. "You want another chair after this week? A week that has proven nothing except that we live in perpetual excess of seating options? Is that what you want me to put down? 'One more chair, please. We don't have enough as it is'? I don't understand. Are you two in cahoots? Is this some sort of coordinated attack to make a fool of me?"

"Oh, sorry." Cline points. "I was just saying there's a chair that we forgot to do."

He's right. At the center of the stage sits a single wooden chair—the only wooden chair we've seen all week—facing forward, looking out over a room of its aluminum-and-plastic relatives.

"I can do it," Gibbs says, and she begins moving to the stage.

"No, I'll do it," I say, but Gibbs does not stop.

It seems clear what is happening: she'd like some sense of moral high ground, to prove that my refusal to fulfill her brazenly stupid wish for a radio will not stop her from doing the work. For this reason, I cannot let her reach the chair before me. And so, aware that I've crossed the line from professionally aggrieved into full-blown pettiness, I walk faster to overtake her. It isn't easy. She's basically already there. I pick up my pace beyond anything that could be considered casual and do a little leap to the stage before she can step up onto it.

I am not an agile man. None of this looks graceful, I'm certain of that. But I'm determined not to betray my lack of sure-footedness by looking at my feet. Instead, I work to maintain what I hope is an expression of purpose as I keep my gaze directly ahead. Because of this, I am looking out the window, straight at the thing in the snow.

What happens in the following second seems to last for an eternity. I am conscious of floating through the air, my eyes on the thing in the snow, until all else fades from sight and it's the only thing I see. The stage, the chair, the room itself—all disappear as a shock of tension seizes my body. My neck has locked in place, and I can't look away. The thing in the snow is there before me, and in that moment, it even seems to be looking back at me. It has no eyes, no expression, but I can sense it harshly judging the whole of my being: my leaping ability, my dexterity, my leadership, my posture, my enunciation, my vocabulary, my wit, the strength of my handshake, everything. I am, for a long moment, nothing more than a soaring conflagration of flaws, many of which remain unidentified even as I feel them rise to the surface of my skin like existential perspiration.

Then, to my surprise, my foot meets the ground. I careen forward unsteadily, feeling a limb tangle with something as I crash to the ground. A loud snap sounds out.

I roll over onto my back as quickly as I can, determined to get up and show the others that I'm okay, but I pause, gazing up at the light fixture directly above me. There does seem to be a slight jitter to its glow, an irregular, almost Morse-like pattern. I tell myself it's just the result of my heart rate being elevated by Gibbs's insolence (not to mention my rush to the stage) before I feel a slight static tingle in my beard. After a few seconds, it aligns itself with the pulse of the light; they almost seem to beat together.

Gibbs arrives first, Cline right after her.

"I seem to have tripped," I say, from the floor.

The others don't reply. They look at me terrified, hesitant to offer a hand.

I push myself up to a sit, which is when I feel something poking my leg. Poking *into* my leg. Or is it *out of* my leg? I fell. Something snapped. Could that have been me? I feel little pain beyond the ache of a bruise forming on my thigh, but I've heard of this happening: of people losing limbs and not realizing it for minutes or even hours, the adrenaline shrouding the full extent of the damage. Fearful of what I might see, I lower my eyes slowly. And there it is: the broken leg. Not my leg. The leg of the chair, snapped in half. Strewn about me lies the rest of it in pieces.

"I guess this one will need replacing," I say, because I need to say something.

"Sure," says Gibbs.

"Totally," says Cline.

They don't look at me. They keep their eyes on the shattered remains of the chair.

11.

The only positive to be taken from the chair's collapse is that it defin-itively ends the conversation concerning Gibbs's potential ra-dio. She does not push the issue further. Instead, she and Cline simply stand there, glancing back and forth between me and the mess I've made, until I tell them that, despite it being be-fore lunch, we're done for the week. I cannot meet their eyes as I speak, and when they wish me a nice weekend, my only reply is a solemn nod.

The extra hours of freedom do little good for me. I spend them in my office, refusing to touch the chair. I stand behind my desk, my legs growing tired, the week's paperwork opened on my desk but not yet filled out.

Chairs requiring replacement: _____

One line to address the hours of sitting and shifting within reason that we have completed. But I cannot bring myself to fill it in, simple as that answer may be. In fact, there is only a single answer, zero, that is simpler than the one that I have to give. I am just one annihilated chair away from perfection.

My mind keeps returning to that moment. The time slowing to a crawl, the strange sense of gravity, the ease with which the seat snapped to pieces—it's as if the thing in the snow folded the world in on itself, weakening the chair, lessening the distance between me and it, and doubling my impact all at once. Clearly, this can't be true. It must have been some combination of frustration and fatigue that warped my perception of what was happening. Moreover, my instinct to blame the thing in the snow, of all things, could even be a defense mechanism, shielding my ego from other, more painful explanations.

Some context here: I am nearly a foot taller than Gibbs, and stand close to five inches over Cline as well. Thus, it is natural that my weight exceeds theirs. And yet, I cannot pretend that my additional heft matches my additional height at a rate of exactly one to one. My size—the width, not the length—is something I've been self-conscious about most of my life. Only here at the Northern Institute have I found some respite. Our aforementioned cold-fighting wardrobe renders all of us equally bulky in appearance. What's more, I can maintain a thick beard with minimal discomfort due to the climate. This hides the gentle slope of my neck, a Pythagorean c-line rather than a strong a-meets-b angle. The result is a general burliness. Like the landscape out the window forever enshrouded by snowy mystery, there's no telling what kind of physique might be hiding under my attire and facial hair.

It is not, however, the simple fact of my size that frustrates me. It is the notion of that size being scrutinized, quantified, and thereafter assessed by doctors, colleagues, and my own bruised psyche, as an error in need of correction. It is in this regard, too, that my time at the Institute has provided me considerable relief. Of course, I can confront myself relentlessly in the shower or the mirror in my suite bathroom, but I did not pack a scale. Just as Kay keeps the Institute's temperature hidden from us, so too do I hide a numerical assessment of my weight; this way, I can't be sure if I have surpassed certain personally significant thresholds, meaningless as they may be.

What happened with the chair does not necessarily change any of this—it's physics, a matter of not just size but also speed and trajectory—but still, to leap so gracelessly and land so forcefully does imply a certain lack of coordination.

Then there's the way the other two looked at me when they finally turned their attention from the wreckage. It was not with genuine concern that I, their supervisor, might be hurt. It was not with the cold indifference of someone doing a task for work, something necessary and devoid of emotional investment. It was not even one of deranged pleasure at seeing me, a figure of some authority, fall on his face. Quite the contrary, Cline and Gibbs looked upon me with nothing but pity. And someone who is in charge should not be pitied by his subordinates.

Finally, there is the issue of noncompliance with the task assigned. I am to report how many chairs require replacement, but implicit in that reportage is that all chairs be assessed according to the guidelines set out for us. Namely, that we shift upon them within reason. To hurtle oneself recklessly at a chair is entirely outside of reason, but this does not change the fact that there's a chair that requires replacement.

In short, I struggle to fill in the blank because until I do, there is no official account of the chair collapsing at all. Previously, I applied Post-its to my paperwork to feel human. Now, I adhere to Kay's policy of limited Post-its like a coward and seek solace in the impersonal nature of the paperwork. I could void an entire week's worth of work—and with it, a single terrible moment—simply by refusing to make any notation at all.

My desk is clear except for the open folder, a mug of pens, and a piece of paper on the corner. This is the page Cline found after we ran into Gilroy earlier this week. I unfold it now and read it to distract myself.

When I was a child, "frostbite" was dangled before me as a threat to ensure I wore proper winter attire when building snowmen or sledding. Being young and naïve and not yet educated in the true but subtle malice with which the cold operates, I envisioned the condition as a set of jagged ice-teeth waiting under the surface of the fresh powder. Impossibly, they could not puncture a set of soft lined mittens, yet could irreparably mangle a bare hand that dug too deep and for too long. But this is exactly what the cold wants. It wants to hide its monopoly on our pain behind a number of shell hurts. It is not the cold's bite but frost's we fear. Just as it is not the dropping temperatures that result in snow falling rather than rain, or sheets of ice forming

*rather than puddles. Instead, we blame the things themselves—
the snow and the ice—for the cold's treachery. I know I did for a
time. But I now see this is the cold's greatest power. When it attacks, it does so with such gusto that we have no time to "follow
the money," so to speak; we can only deal with whatever form it
takes in its current onslaught. When it does not attack, it registers only as a vague sense of dread. We can think of times so cold
we shivered, times so frigid it seemed like our facial muscles took
a full minute to return to their resting positions after each blink.
We can recall blizzards erasing everything and everyone unlucky
enough to be caught in their fury. We can remember slipping on
ice, can even perhaps recall the pain that persisted where we hit
the ground. But it is impossible to reinhabit the feeling of help-
lessness that comes with the cold after it has receded.*

It continues from here, but I struggle to keep reading. I'm
not sure I entirely agree with the premise, and also Gilroy's
writing grows more abstract as it goes, losing me. Plus, the bit
about the pain seems to activate the faint ache in my own thigh,
which returns me to the task at hand: the paperwork.

I don't look out the window—I won't let myself, not after
what doing so did to me earlier—but I can tell night has fallen.
A single lamp in the corner lights the room.

The time has come. After reviewing and subsequently re-
hiding the snow sickness symptom card as a matter of course
(there are, unfortunately, no boxes to check for rampant distraction and baseless speculation), I take a deep breath and I
fill in the blank with a *1*. I then take another deep breath and
make my way to the roof, stopping at my quarters to don my

cold-weather clothes. The air shocks me, but fails to serve its usual function of separating the workday from the weekend.

Back in my room, I have a case of fortified wine. I've opened only a single bottle and poured myself a glass once before, after a week of moving desks in windowed offices to opposite sides of the facility (to ensure even sun-fading, Kay explained) during which I tweaked something in my back. This week, it is not only pain but frustration that I hope to smooth over as I uncork the bottle. But try as I might, I can't take my mind off the day's happenings. When I am at last bundled under my covers taking small sips, I hear the helicopter approach, pause, and retreat, and all I can think of is the news of the broken chair flying toward Kay. Such a contrast to the week before, when I needed no fortified wine at all, when the thrill of writing the Post-it had been an intoxication unto itself.

Then it occurs to me: Kay's response, concerning the identity of the thing in the snow, will be in this week's folder of assignments.

I gulp down the rest of my fortified wine and pour a second glass, this one to celebrate. I have the urge to rush to the roof this instant and collect the folder, but I quickly decide against it. This is no time to change course. I will remain steadfast in my ways, and only hope that my anticipation of that knowledge Kay has provided can buoy me until Monday.

12.

Another weekend at the Northern Institute.

Try as I might to suppress it, the workweek's horrible conclusion registers in some small ways.

I find myself eating my provisions with less excitement than usual, and walking with more vigor. Twice, I take to the stairwell, and both times I end up walking all the way to the top, where I stand facing the door to the roof, thinking of the paperwork in its weatherproof lockbox, and the note from Kay that will snuff out any lingering concern about the thing in the snow and return us to some semblance of normalcy.

At some other point, perhaps after my trips to the roof's door, or maybe before, I complete several laps around the first floor. At first, I walk at a leisurely pace, hoping to keep my heart rate steady so that its throb does not once again seem to mimic the pulse of the lights (which I still don't fully believe is there). But I grow impatient and begin to seek the burn of exertion, picking up my stride to the point that I am nearly jogging for several laps. Soon I find myself out of breath. My legs quake with exhaustion, and I need to sit down. This should not be a difficult task—we have just confirmed that the first two floors of the Institute are a veritable wellspring of stable seating options—but the last time I attempted to sit in a chair, I destroyed it, so I remain in the hallway, resting my back against the wall and sliding down slowly to a seated position upon the muted green tile. It's cold, but I remain this way for some time.

I'm on book ten of the Leader series: *A Country Retreat*. Jack French has traveled to a countryside meadow where vacationers can rent small, single-room cabins. It should be serene, the perfect place in which to finally put into words his essential treatise on management. It is, unfortunately, anything but. In the center of the semicircle of cabins, there is a cluster of picnic tables where a group of men and women from the other cabins convene daily to argue. Each morning, they bring notepads to record their progress, and at the end of each day they depart back to their cabins, fuming, their pages blank.

Jack French observes this all. The days are warmer than expected for October, and the cabins lack air-conditioning, so he must write with his window open. But the group's bickering keeps him from making any substantial progress. When he confronts them one day, asking for a bit of peace, he finds out they are engineers. They've recently been provided a grant by a major agricultural company to "reimagine traditional grain storage." Much like Jack French himself, they've sought this place out hoping to really dive into their work. Only, now that they have the backing, they do not know where to start, fearful to get off going in the wrong direction.

Shortly after this confrontation, the countryside is over-taken by a militant group of religious fundamentalists, dead set on the eradication of all science. They manage to destroy the cars in the lot at the meadow's base, so Jack French has no choice but to flee with the engineers on foot. Eventually, given that it's fall, they come to a corn maze. Seeing no other way forward, they enter, and quickly arrive at a dead end. The engineers panic, but Jack French reassures them that dead ends are a crucial part of any maze, if not the characteristic that makes a maze difficult and exciting. If you do not meet some dead ends, he explains, the maze was not worth the undertaking. This ends up being a lesson the engineers apply later, in the book's epilogue, when the militia has been de-feated and they have successfully reimagined modern grain storage. At the unveiling ceremony for their ambitious new silo, they thank Jack French profusely, but of course, he isn't present. He's off somewhere else, attempting to complete his masterwork.

Beyond the final page is a photo of the author, Rodney Stuyvesant Jr. In it, he has thinning hair and large, thick-framed glasses, and wears a jacket and tie. He does not smile. Below his photo, his biographical note reads:

It is simple and to the point, much like my own biographical note would be, except for a very different reason; while Rodney Stuyvesant Jr. has experienced so much success that he must summarize it broadly, mine would be short due to a lack of worthy material to report. Viewed this way, success appears not as exponential growth but as a bell curve, the path from a simplicity that hides nothing to a simplicity that encompasses everything.

At some point early on, we found a dead leaf from a long-gone plant in one of the rooms, prompting Cline to call it "the Garden." The result was immediate. Even after we discarded the leaf, rendering the room nearly identical to the rest, the space seemed to take on a personality. We might lose track of where we were in the building, but we always knew when we were in the Garden.

After that, we looked for any opportunity to name the rooms. There is the room we found the tennis ball in, which we call "the Court." There is the room that inexplicably had a mirror hanging on the wall, which we call "the Vanity." There is the windowless room with shelves lining the walls, which we refer to as "the Library" (although sometime later Gibbs observed that, given its proximity to one of the small kitchens throughout the Institute, it was probably a pantry). There are others, too, where the characteristics that deemed them name-worthy were so small that we no longer remember them. The room we refer to as "Cold Storage," for example, is no colder than any other room on the fourth floor. Nor is "the Sauna" on the fifth floor any warmer than its neighboring interior rooms. In other words, the rooms have become known for their names, rather than named for why we know them.

On some of my weekend walks, I make it a game to visit each of the rooms we've named. And it is in this way that I find myself standing in the doorway to the room just a few doors down from my office on the third floor, which we call "the Lookout" for reasons I cannot recall. Unlike many of the other forgotten rooms, its name seems not just unearned, but wrong. After all, its third-floor location is a poor lookout point. Wouldn't a room on the fourth or fifth floor provide more dis-tant views, thanks to its elevation? Then, of course, there is the enormous wall of glass in the seventh-floor amphitheater. And none of this takes into account the same basic issue that makes the wall of glass so strange in the first place: the idea of a lookout implies there being something worthwhile to look out upon, but no such view exists here.

Until now. Standing in the doorway, I see that the Lookout's windows perfectly frame the thing in the snow; sitting in its bed of white, it occupies the exact center of the middle pane. Its features appear clearer, and it somehow looks even larger, from this angle than from my office, no more than a hundred feet away.

Here is the thought that disturbs me most: What if we had no previous reason for naming this room the Lookout? By which I mean, what if that name, when we bestowed it upon the anonymous room, was predictive rather than descriptive? What if calling it by that name foretold the thing in the snow's invasion into our lives? This is impossible, of course. But as I stare into the room for a long time, trying to recall what detail inspired the nomenclature, nothing else comes to mind.

Eventually, I walk away.

As I may have mentioned before, Friday nights at the Northern Institute feel distinct, as they usher in the weekend, and Sunday nights feel distinct, as they lead me back to structure. It would follow, then, that Saturday nights should also feel distinct, as any night experienced between Friday night and Sunday night would, as a rule, be a Saturday night. But now I can't be sure. The memories of any given moment on the weekend fade as soon as they're created, and often there's no telling what time it is, clocks be damned. What feels like a walk I'm taking early Saturday morning, before sunrise, might actually be happening late Saturday night. Or early Saturday night, after the gray of day fades to the darker gray of evening, or even Sunday morning, or the moments after sunset late on Sunday afternoon, immediately before Sunday night, the official harbinger of work, fully crystallizes and my normal sense of time returns. Likewise, I'm unsure if I sleep between Saturday morning and Sunday evening, except in a series of naps whose varying lengths escape me. Whenever I try to reconstruct the weekend's order of events, I find each memory fringed with a sleepiness that could be one of having just awoken or one of needing to lie down.

The things that remain in order are those dictated by logic. Taking the stairs down to the first floor must precede doing a lap of the first floor; therefore, I remember it that way. And I have no problem reconstructing the sequence of a given book in the Leader series, not to mention the sequence of the books themselves. I know Jack French acquired the church key can opener from the team of brewers at the ropes course in book three, only to misplace it in book five, and find it again, in a pair of shorts he'd not worn in some time, in book eight, so that he can use it to puncture a discreet lens-sized hole in the wall of his rustic thatched beach hut to photograph two rival coffee executives shaking hands after agreeing to an illegal sale of farmland. It's the broader order that eludes me: Did I walk the first floor before reading, or the other way around? The connective moments—the naps, the times drinking tea and sitting quietly—seem to be what muddles everything, so that each weekend resembles a jumbled bin of fully formed episodes, not a neatly ordered stack.

Is this something I should be reporting on the snow sickness symptom card? Kay told me I shouldn't need to fill one out as long as I don't go out onto the snow, but could what I experience on the weekends be that same disorder seeping in through the thick glass windows, permeating the rooms of the Northern Institute just like the cold?

This is what I am thinking about when, suddenly, things seem to lock into place and a sensation of clarity befalls me, banishing all thought of the card. Sunday night has arrived. Work awaits, just a few short hours away. I'd better get some sleep.

In this way, another weekend at the Northern Institute passes.

13.

When the cold blasts me as I step out onto the roof Monday morning, I'm already so excited that I feel the desire to skip. Ultimately, with some concentration and a breathing exercise made painful by the sharp air, this giddiness is quelled.

I unload the provisions first, before removing the folder from the lockbox along with a small plastic bag containing three golf balls. Their purpose will be made clear by the folder, I'm sure, and I shove them into my pocket so I can grip the folder tightly in both hands. It's as if it radiates electricity. I can feel it as a low buzz in the base of my beard.

At our morning coffee, I forgo any light socialization because I can barely speak. Cline, more chipper than usual, makes up for my silence.

"I spent a lot of time standing this weekend," Cline says. "Felt nice. After all that sitting last week. Good for the back."

He talks to neither of us directly, but glances from Gibbs to me.

"Hmm," I say.

"Interesting," Gibbs says.

I can tell that the brief flash of pity she felt for me, as I lay sprawled across the floor among the debris of the collapsed chair, has faded. She's angry now, likely because I dismissed her radio request. I do not feel the burn of this anger, though; I experience even greater excitement for our coffee hour to expire so that I can bring an end to the all-too-enticing mystery of the thing in the snow.

Soon enough, the time comes. I set down my mug and lift the folder from my desk, holding it for long enough to draw both Cline's and Gibbs's eyes. Still, I don't speak. I want them to initiate, to demand an explanation for my silence. Yes, I've been an accommodating supervisor thus far, allowing them to take coffee and light socialization for granted, but I will not compromise on this. I need them to ask me why I'm remaining quiet so that I know I can gain and hold their undivided attention through means beyond agility-related humiliation.

"So, what are we doing this week?" Cline asks finally.

Good enough.

"We'll get to that soon enough," I say. "First, there's something that must be addressed. I've noticed a disturbing trend over the last week and several days: a willingness among certain parties on our team to give themselves over to distraction and reckless speculation, specifically that concerning the object that Cline spotted in the snow." Simply speaking of its existence draws their twin gazes to the window, and I must speak louder to return their attention to me. "I understand its appeal. We've

71

never seen a thing nestled in the snow before. All previous views from this office have been of a never-ending sea of white. And while I recognize that there is a certain excitement in the unknown, we've let it distract us from the important work Kay has given us to do."

"Did we really?" Gibbs asks.

"What?"

"Did we really let it distract us? We were just sitting."

"And shifting," Cline adds. "Within reason."

"We were ensuring the stability of the chairs," I say. "If a team of researchers were to arrive next week—"

"A team of researchers is arriving next week?" Cline says.

"No," I say. "No one is arriving next week. But, hypothetically, were there to be, and were they to gather on the seventh floor for an important introductory meeting concerning the work to come—"

"So they're *new* researchers," Cline says.

"What?" I say.

"You said 'introductory meeting,'" Cline says, "which would mean it's not the researchers who were here before. Otherwise, it would be more of a refresher."

"It doesn't matter whether they're new or not," I say.

"The more details the better, with hypotheticals," Cline says. "For me at least."

"Fine," I say. "Let's say they're new researchers. And at this introductory meeting, they all attempt to take their seats, only for some subtle jockeying to escalate into full-scale bumps and pushes that send researchers stumbling into the chairs, causing them to collapse en masse—"

"Or there could be a wet floor," Cline interjects.

"What?"

"Just seems like a wet-floor situation is more plausible," Cline says. "Everyone's just arrived, they want to get things off to a good start, so someone mops the floor but forgets to put out the yellow sandwich board. Next thing you know, researchers are coming in, and they're coming in hot, excited to get things going. And it's like an ice rink in there, people sliding everywhere, losing their balance, just mowing down chairs left and right."

"Fine," I say. "The mass collapse of chairs is initiated due to a recently mopped floor and inadequate signage."

Cline nods. "Thank you. This is really clicking for me now."

"This would reflect very poorly on us," I go on, "and, in turn, on Kay, for bestowing upon us the responsibility of ensuring the steadfastness of the chairs. Not to mention, it would result in a fair share of pain, frustration, and embarrassment."

I leave a pause for the two of them to silently acknowledge that I speak of these things from experience.

Gibbs is unconcerned with my feelings. "But what I was saying is that wouldn't happen. Because we *did* check the structural stability of the chairs. And we finished by lunch on Friday, so we couldn't have been too distracted by whatever's out there in the snow."

"A fair point," I admit. "We couldn't have been too distracted by whatever's out there in the snow. Yet. But in the coming weeks, we may be given tasks that do not allow us to simply sit and stare at it while shifting our weight."

"Within reason," Cline says.

"Exactly," I say. "We may have tasks that draw our attention away from the windows entirely, tasks that require the kind of intense focus and teamwork that do not allow for a wandering eye. But this will not be an issue. As the supervisor of our small team, I have taken it upon myself to solve the riddle that is the thing in the snow."

"Wait, did you go out there?" Gibbs says. "I thought we weren't allowed on the snow."

"It is not exploration, but rather foresight, that will give us the answer," I say. "The very first day we saw the thing in the snow, I put pen to paper and asked Kay what it might be. Given the delay of the helicopter visits, that means the response will be in this week's assignments."

"Will be?" Cline says. "You haven't read it?"

"Not yet," I say. "As with every week, I do not look at the assignments before Monday so that we can experience them as a team." I await some acknowledgment of the collaborative mood this encourages, but none comes, so I open the folder, standing there, behind my desk. On the sheet of assignments, sure enough, is a Post-it, Kay's response.

H.,
Re: thing in snow. Unsure. Need more info.
—K.

"So," Cline asks. "What is it?"

"She doesn't know," I say, as all the morning's excitement curdles into nausea.

"She can't identify it?" Try as she might, Gibbs cannot fully hide how much this possibility thrills her.

"It's not that," I say. "She just needs more information."

"Well, what did you tell her?" Cline asks.

"I told her there was a thing," I say, "in the snow."

"And?" Gibbs says.

"That's it." The pulse running through my beard has gone from giddy to malevolent. It mocks me and makes my face feel warm and sick. "But no bother. I'll provide a bit more detail in my next correspondence."

"But you barely even look at it," Gibbs says.

"Excuse me?" I say.

"We should do it," Gibbs says, indicating herself and Cline with a gesture of her head.

"You two?" I say. "Without me?"

"I mean, if you'd like to help," Cline offers.

Gibbs ignores this. As she speaks, she moves to refresh her mug. "You've just finished telling us about how we've been distracted by it, therefore implying that you yourself haven't paid it any attention. If that's the case, wouldn't it be making the best of what you seem to think is a bad situation to use our distraction to the advantage of the team by having us describe the thing in the snow for Kay?"

I take a long drink of my coffee, cold by now, to buy some time, but I cannot muster a response. The issue here is that Gibbs is right—I've walked right into this thanks to my sanctimonious prologue in which I touted my immunity to the thing in the snow's pull as a strength—but I can't admit as much. There's a difference between a supervisor delegating and a subordinate taking whatever task they please.

"Kay expects messages to come from me," I say. "I'll take some time after work today, give it a closer look, and put together a more thorough description."

Gibbs crosses her arms, the white of her mug peeking out from behind her shoulder. "You'll take some time after work today? That's all you think you'll need?"

"Why would it take longer than that?" I ask.

Gibbs lets out an exasperated sigh, and I have never felt more disrespected. I might say something that is neither light nor social (which would be warranted, given both Gibbs's level of disrespect and the fact that our discussion has carried us past nine in the morning, and thus out of the time for coffee and light socialization) if it weren't for Cline's interjection.

"That's actually a good point," he says.

"It is?" Gibbs says.

"What point?" I say.

"The time," Cline says. "If someone takes a long time observing a thing and the other person doesn't, that's not necessarily an indication of which one will be better at describing it. What actually matters is who's the best at writing descriptions."

"And how do you tell that?" Gibbs asks.

Cline considers this for a moment, and then offers, "We could do a contest. A description contest."

Gibbs does not like this idea, I can tell, but she still looks at me with eyes that ask, *Well?* The office falls into a silence interrupted only by the sound of coffee pouring into my mug.

I find the energy I had just an hour ago depleted. In the time it takes for my cup to fill, I run the figurative numbers: while I would prefer to begin working, I can tell that my vetoing of the description contest and taking the task for myself will result in a cold and likely inefficient work environment. Furthermore, there's another danger to consider. If, after causing such friction and writing my own description of the thing in the snow, I were to receive word from Kay that she still did not know what it was, this would be quite the blow to my authority, perhaps even more embarrassing than the collapsing chair.

So, despite the fact that we've entered work hours and we have yet to even look at the task for the week, I say, "Fine. We'll do a contest."

14.

"We could each describe that," Cline says, and he points to the lamp in the corner of my office.

When we'd arrived at the Northern Institute, one of the first jobs Kay gave us was to gather any personal items left behind by the researchers and move them to a closet on the first floor. We'd found a number of things: some dry-erase markers, a photo of the entire research team, a number of bracelets that all seemed the same except some had a pendant with a gold letter *S* and some had a pendant with a bronze letter *T*, a T-shirt from something called "The Chlorine Conference," an old mousetrap jerry-rigged to work as a cigarette lighter, a peacock feather encased in a clear sealant with a strap attached for hanging, lanyards innumerable. Altogether, a variety of truly random ephemera.

I'd found the lamp in an empty room in my living suite, and rather than depositing it with the other items, I brought it here, to my office, thinking it might lend the room a homier glow than the harsh overheads on darker mornings. It is by no means an ornate piece, but compared to the plainness of the rest of the furniture in the office, it stands out, making it the only possible subject for our contest, so Gibbs and I agree.

"But we need some parameters," Cline says. "Like, you can't say 'lamp.'"

"Why not?" I ask.

"Because we don't even know what sort of *thing* the thing in the snow is," Cline says. "So we're basically doing a two-tiered description: one tier is the broader category of thing and the second is the actual thing. In other words, with the lamp, if someone were to read your description and say, 'Sounds like a lamp,' that's good but not ideal, since there are so many kinds of lamps. Tall ones. Short ones. Ones with long bulbs. The ones that have the green shade thing, like in libraries. The old-timey kind with handles that run on gas."

"Lanterns," I say.

"I've heard them called lamps," Gibbs says.

"Basically, if you end up with a description of 'a thing that does light,' that's not enough." Cline points to the lamp again. "We want to try and describe it in such a way that it could be only *that* thing that does light."

"So if I wanted to say about the lamp——" I start to say, seeking some clarity, but Cline cuts me off.

"Use the coffee machine," he says.

"What?" I say. "I thought we were describing the lamp."

Cline gestures to the coffee machine. "Just for your example of what you would say, I mean, use that. That way, you won't give away any of your ideas about how you're going to describe the lamp."

"I don't mind if someone else wants to use the example of what I have to say about the lamp," I say.

"I do," Gibbs says.

"What?" I say.

"What if you describe the lamp in a way that isn't good?" Gibbs says.

"Then you don't have to use it," I say.

"But it might get stuck in our heads," Gibbs says. "Like, if you were to say 'warming circle,' that might edge out better potential ways of saying it, because now we're all thinking of it as a 'warming circle.'"

"'Warming circle,'" I say. "You mean the bulb?"

"I was using the coffee machine," Gibbs says.

"The hot plate part," Cline clarifies.

"Thank you," Gibbs says.

"No, thank *you*," Cline says. "'Warming circle' is exactly the kind of stuff we're looking for in this exercise, if it were about a coffee machine and not a lamp."

"Okay," I say. "So if I wanted to say about the coffee machine—"

"Only, you can't say 'coffee machine,' in this hypothetical," Cline says.

"Right," I say, but then fall silent as the example I was initially going to put forward had to do with the lamp, and I have not spent any time thinking about the coffee machine.

"You'd say something like, 'The bulb fills slowly with an energizing elixir,'" Cline offers.

"I thought we weren't supposed to talk about the lamp right now," I say.

"He's talking about the carafe," Gibbs says. "Which is bulbous in shape."

"Thank you," Cline says. "But also, case in point to what Gibbs was saying: you say 'bulb' and in my head I'm like, 'Oh, great, there's a word to use: bulb.' Anyway, does that clear things up?"

"Sure," I lie.

And so the terms are decided: we will write a description of the lamp (not the coffee machine) without using the word "lamp," in order to decide who will write a description of the thing in the snow, a thing we do not know the name of, this being what the description hopes to solve, in both broad and specific terms.

I have some notebooks and pens that I dispense, and we take our seats. I sit at my desk, easing into position in a slow way that, I hope, conveys a man overwhelmed by a certain lamp's descriptive possibilities, not someone exercising excessive caution after his last attempt to sit in a chair failed spectacularly. Cline sets up on the other side, kneeling in a way that must be uncomfortable. Gibbs takes an extra chair in the corner to the small side table where the coffee machine is. I set a timer for twenty minutes on a stopwatch (provided for some previous week's task that I no longer recall) and the contest begins.

This duration seemed, when Cline suggested it, to be an interminably long time, but now, as I put pen to paper, I find the word "lamp" has gained a nearly unbearable magnetism. The fact that I'm forbidden from using the word renders it the most alluring word in the English language, and I have to fight my desire to attach it to every other part of the lamp: not a base, but a *lamp* base; not a socket, but a *lamp* socket. The entire room rearranges itself in my mind, a solar system of chairs and desks and employees, each definable primarily by its proximity and relationship to the lamp.

It takes a great mental effort to follow the rules as they've been laid out, and the allotted time passes quickly. When I finish, I look at the stopwatch, expecting that only a few minutes have ticked by, and watch the final fifteen seconds deplete. Gibbs writes diligently, glancing up at the lamp occasionally, whereas Cline seems to be swiping his pen across his sheet of paper in a wild motion that cannot possibly be producing words. When the beep sounds, indicating time is up, he flinches and looks around the room as if coming out of a trance, before his eyes return to his paper.

"Oh no," he says.

"What is it?" I ask.

Out of the corner of my eye, I notice Gibbs hesitating. She glances first at Cline and then at me, but does not seem to sense my attention. Believing herself to be unobserved, she quickly writes a few more words before putting her pen down with a forcefulness that betrays her guilt.

"I did a drawing," Cline explains.

"You drew the lamp?" I say.

"Sort of. It's a thing I do," Cline says. "Since I work best in a visual medium, I'll often do some sketching to get my thoughts in order, before writing things down. It can be an issue. I've gone through an entire sketch pad and been like, 'Wait, what was I doing?' And then it's like, 'Oh yeah. Making a grocery list.'"

"So you started sketching and lost track of time," I say.

"Exactly," Cline says.

"Can I see it?" I ask.

Cline slides the paper across the desk to me. A number of lines weave together to form something I can't quite discern. "This is the lamp?"

"It's one man's interpretation of the lamp," Cline says.

"But it's not the actual lamp," I say.

"It is and it isn't," Cline says. "That happens sometimes in art."

"What does this mean for the contest?" Gibbs asks.

It's a good question. Cline considers it for a moment.

"I guess, well, if my entry is ineligible, then I should probably be the judge."

"The judge," I say.

"Yeah," he says. "Since there are two of you and two descriptions."

"So," I say, "you'll decide who is the best describer of the lamp."

"Exactly," Cline says.

I have been so preoccupied with Gibbs's various attempts to seize some modicum of power and somehow it's Cline who swoops in to assert control over the entire present situation. That he's able to take charge due to an utter failure of participation—rendering, upon the page, a hackneyed image and not a single word to describe a lamp—makes it even bolder, and honestly, I'm more impressed than offended.

"Okay," I say. "You can judge."

"Agreed," Gibbs says.

We both hand our descriptions to Cline, who places them on the floor, looking from one paper to the next, his face contorted in a crude impression of Gilroy caught in the throes of a deep, troubled thought. I check the clock over the door and find it's nearly ten. We need to start working, and I hope for a swift conclusion to Cline's judging. He takes nearly a half hour as Gibbs and I sit, silently.

"Well, it was close," Cline says, finally, "but ultimately, I went with this one." He holds up one of the pages.

"Whose is it?" I ask.

"I don't know," Cline says. "I judged blindly."

"How does it start?" Gibbs asks.

Cline lowers the paper and reads the first line. "'In the corner of the office—'"

"That's mine," Gibbs says, an audacious assertion, really, that the decision to locate the lamp would be one unique to her.

"I just felt very grounded in this," Cline goes on. "I wasn't like, 'Okay, that's just a lamp.' I was like, 'That's a lamp that exists in a place, for a purpose.' This one—" He holds up the other page.

"Hart's," Gibbs says.

"Mine," I say.

"I just felt a little lost," Cline says, turning to me. "It was very clinical, and uncentered. You were so set on establishing the basics that you didn't give yourself over to the subject matter and consider what kind of space it carves out in the world. I kept thinking, 'Where is this thing?' You know what I mean? Like, it could just as easily be in here as it could be out there." He points out the window.

"Wouldn't that be a good thing?" I say. "After all, the thing in the snow is out in the snow."

Cline opens his mouth but does not speak. Gibbs crosses her arms. I have gone too far, I realize. An unspoken aspect of the agreement was that we would not argue with Cline's verdict.

"Could I see them both?" I say, an attempt at changing course.

Cline looks at Gibbs. She nods, and Cline hands me the papers. I skim Gibbs's description and my suspicions are confirmed: the ending wraps things up perfectly, an ending that would not have been possible had I forgone listening to Cline blather on about sketching to gather his thoughts and simply called her out for going over time in the moment. Nevertheless, I cannot raise this issue now. She would simply deny it. But I do notice one other thing that seems worth mentioning.

"You say 'shade,'" I say.

Gibbs looks at the lamp and back at me. "It has a shade."

"But it's kind of a giveaway, isn't it?" I say. "What else has a shade?"

"Windows have shades," Gibbs offers.

"It's also something that trees do," Cline says.

"Also, a shade is a separate part," Gibbs says, her voice rising ever so slightly. "They're detachable and sometimes sold separately."

"Oh man, are they ever," Cline says. "Learned that one the hard way. A few times."

It becomes suddenly apparent that I need to be done with this, and there is one way to be done with it as quickly as possible. I place the papers down on the desk and stand. The others do too. "Well," I say to Gibbs, "congratulations."

She seems suspicious but accepts my concession. When I move out from behind my desk, she moves quickly into my place.

"What are you doing?" I ask.

"I'm going to describe the thing in the snow," she says.

"Here?" I say. "The Lookout has a better view."

"I think I'll be more disciplined if I have a good desk to sit at," she says.

"But it isn't even facing the window," I say. "You'll have to turn around and look over your shoulder every time you want to see it."

"I can manage," Gibbs says.

"And you're going to work on it now," I say, "during the workday? How long do you think it will take?"

"You need it by the end of the week, right?" Gibbs says, pulling her chair in and readying herself to write.

I realize two things at once: first, that Gibbs would like to spend the entire week describing the thing in the snow; and, second, after all of this, I would very much like to spend the week apart from Gibbs.

"End of the week should work perfectly," I say, and she takes her seat.

15.

The purpose of the golf balls, it turns out, is to measure flatness. According to the paperwork provided, we are to proceed through the rooms and ensure "a continued flatness of surfaces where flatness would be required" by placing golf balls upon them. If the golf ball can remain still, that means the surface is flat. If the golf ball rolls, that means the surface is not level and we should report this.

"Surfaces," Cline says, after I read him our instructions. We're in a room on the first floor, the one we call "the Cubicle," again. "So, like, tables?"

"Certainly," I say.

"Desks," Cline says.

"Yes," I say.

"Windowsills?" Cline asks.

"I don't think we need to worry about windowsills," I say, "given they're less likely to be used in the research process."

"The floor?" Cline says. "Or, wait, I guess if all the tables and desks check out as flat, that would mean the floors are flat too."

"That's a good point," I say. "We can inspect the floor in the event of a rolling golf ball."

"But not chairs," Cline says.

"I think we've done enough with chairs," I say.

"Plus they're not entirely flat," Cline says.

"Yes," I say.

"Because of the groove on the butt part," Cline says.

"I understood," I say.

With that, I hand Cline a golf ball, take one for myself, and pocket the third. Cline moves to test the flatness of a desk. I step to a long conference table and freeze.

It has been a long morning, and we are finally, just now, starting to work. We need to make up for lost time, but I cannot bring myself to begin. After everything that's already transpired—my grandiose lead-in to a letdown of a Post-it, being bested by Gibbs, ceding my desk, which is to say nothing of last week's dismal conclusion—fear sends a tremor through my hands. Fear that the ball will not rest. Fear that failure is simply my lot in life. And furthermore, fear that the failure will be one of user error. Or, even worse, that the source of the failure will be unknowable, that I will proceed through the week trying and failing to both bring a golf ball to stillness on a flat surface and assess its reason for unrest, until finally there is nothing to do but choose: Do I blame myself, and report that the tables are flat, or do I find fault in the table? Either outcome possesses exceptional downsides.

On the one hand, a table incorrectly assessed as "flat" could result in a number of costly accidents, if research is to ever resume. I imagine a scenario in which an expensive piece of equipment is set to rest on a supposedly flat table. It makes slow, undetectable progress toward the edge, eventually falling to the ground, where it is damaged or destroyed. And if the researchers are lucky, this will happen in plain sight. Were it to happen in the evening, with no witnesses present, someone would simply arrive in the morning to find their station vandalized. A culprit would be sought out. Rifts would develop. Tensions might rise, distracting the researchers from their work. Mistakes would be made. As for the other potential outcome—perfectly flat tables wrongly assessed due to a clumsiness of my hand—the repercussions would be unnecessary expenditure for Kay and unnecessary labor for us.

Making matters worse, the division of our group increases the number of tables I will personally assess. Were Gibbs here, and were she a more steady hand with a golf ball than I— something she would love knowing, I should add—our risk factor would be lowered considerably. All of this seems like a perfectly good reason to climb the three sets of stairs, walk into the office—*my* office—and place a golf ball on the desk (or maybe hand it to her, lest it roll, thus shedding light on this being a decision made out of fear rather than authority) and demand that Gibbs come with us, to complete the task Kay has assigned. And if she would like to write a description of the thing in the snow, that's fine, but it can be done in the evening, after five, as a more permeable barrier between work time and free time is one of the burdens of a supervisor's responsibility.

"Desk is flat," Cline says, bringing my attention back to reality.

I turn and find him standing next to it, pointing to a stilled golf ball.

"Oh," I say. "Good."

"How's yours?" he asks. It's a generous way to phrase the question, considering how I must look, standing next to the table, gripping the golf ball in my hand like I'm trying to squeeze juice from it.

"I was just thinking," I say, "with such a long table, where's the best place to put the ball down?"

"Why don't we each take a side," Cline suggests, another act of charity, as the table being flat on one side and slanted on the other seems improbable. Still, we move to either end, pushing our way through a sea of chairs to get there. Cline lays his ball down, steadies it, and then lifts his hand, leaving it unmoving. I imitate his moves, concentrating to steady the slight quake in my hand, an act that only accentuates it, but still the ball remains where I've placed it after I've released my hold.

"Seems flat," I say.

"Table's good," Cline says.

A weight lifts from me, and we move on. The rest of the morning proceeds smoothly, no noise but the ambient hum of the Institute, the shuffle of our feet between tables, and the soft click of a golf ball being delicately set down, followed by the announcement of "flat" or "good" or, when I desire to lend the work a more official tenor, "table assessed." We talk about nothing else, and there is a convivial warmth to the quiet efficiency with which we work. Over the course of the day, my concerns from the morning fade almost entirely, so much so that when I place my golf ball upon a round table and it refuses to sit still, but rather rolls slowly around the table's perimeter before reversing course and coming back, I do not consider for a moment that it could be an issue of user error.

"We've got a defect," I announce to Cline, and he moves from the long table in the corner to come watch as I reapply my golf ball. Once again it moves as if to inspect the table's edge before retreating.

"Why's it doing that?" Cline says.

"The table's not flat," I say.

"But why would it come back?" he says.

"I don't know," I say, and it strikes me that Cline is right: this is not a normal way for a golf ball to act, even one placed upon a sloped surface. And though I have not been paying close attention to our path, and though we are on the first floor and I cannot look out the window to confirm, I feel absolutely certain what side of the building we are on. My mouth goes dry and my beard throbs with new fervor as I wait for Cline to tie this, in some way, to the thing in the snow.

Instead, what he says is: "Did you put spin on it?"

"What?" I say. "No."

"Put it down again," Cline says, which I do. "I think I saw you put some spin on it."

"I did not put any spin on it," I say.

"That's not what I'm seeing," Cline says.

"But why?" I say. "Why would I put spin on it?"

Cline shrugs. "You might not have done it consciously. It is a golf ball, i.e., something to be played with. And putting spin on a ball is a playful thing to do. So maybe your brain is like, 'Oh nice, a ball, I gotta play with this thing.'"

"But even if I did put spin on it"—just admitting the possibility feels like self-betrayal—"how would I make it do this?" I place the ball down again, and for the fourth time it completes its rotation and doubles back.

"I went to a live painting event once," Cline says. "Guy had converted a pool table into a workstation. Each pocket was filled with paint remover. So, he'd take a suggestion from the audience, like 'pumpkin patch' or something. Then he'd take the cue ball, dip it in wet paint, and knock it around the table on the paper he'd laid down, doing these expert strokes. He'd even jump the ball into the pockets when he needed to clean it but didn't want another stroke across the painting. At first, everyone would be like, 'What's this guy doing?' But then over time, it would be like, 'Oh damn, that's a pumpkin patch.'"

"What does that have to do with anything?" I ask.

"I'm just saying," Cline says, "there's all kinds of spin."

"So the pool painter used spin is your point?" I say.

"A pumpkin is a rounded gourd," Cline explains. "How could you not use spin to render the sides?" He waits for some acknowledgment, but I can think of nothing to say. He sighs. "Look, what are your associations with golf balls?"

"My associations," I say.

"When you see this"—he holds up his own golf ball in front of my eyes—"what's the first memory that comes to mind?"

This simple question stumps me. I am not a golfer, but I am an adult man with managerial aspirations, so it seems impossible that I have never golfed. I can find no memory of golfing, though, nor of engaging in any of its miniature or lesser varieties. Moreover, the idea of thinking back to a time pre-Institute upsets my stomach in an inexplicable way. Eventually I am able to pull one vague recollection of using a golf ball to relieve some arch pain in my left foot. I recount this to Cline, feeling certain that this will put an end to the argument, as the golf ball's use in this memory is one of utility, not sport, much like in our current situation. But Cline only nods sagely. "A rolling motion," he says. "Spin."

"Fine," I say. "If you're so certain I've put spin on my ball, why don't you try?"

Cline places his ball on the table. It sits completely still.

This should really be the end of it. I should cut my losses and move on before falling victim to pettifoggery. But, for some reason, I can't help it: I have to put my ball down again. It rolls, knocking into Cline's ball along its way, which, for its part, wobbles and then returns to rest.

Cline watches my ball move with an exhausted expression. "You know what, why don't I take a look underneath," he says, as if the table is something with an engine on which further diagnostic tests can be run.

He gets to his knees and cranes his neck to look underneath. I remain standing, an attempt to reassert some authority.

"Whoa," he says, after just a moment. "What the hell?"

My heart races. "A structural issue?"

Cline does not stand back up. "No," he says, moving farther under the table. "Writing. Like, lots of it."

16.

Cline is right. The underside of the table is covered with writing. Dense blocks of it—some facing this way, some facing the other—in a variety of handwritings. Cline and I crawl under the table and read the most legible entries, finding that much of it amounts to anonymous confessions.

One author discusses a cactus they once had. They kept it at their desk at a previous place of employment and gave it a pet name, but did not tell anyone, as their position, another one in the field of research, demanded a whimsy-free approach to all they encountered. Once, they referred to the cactus by name in the presence of another researcher. When that researcher asked, politely, what they had just said, the author panicked and made up an explanation about the name belonging to the variety of cactus. For months following the reaction, they lived with two equivalent fears: that the lie would be discovered, and also, paradoxically, that it wouldn't be, that it would seep out into the greater world, spreading further and further by casual conversations involving cacti, and that they, the author, one who has made a career in the pursuit of ultimate truths through research, would be responsible for a falsehood.

Another author writes that they enjoy bluegrass music, but cannot bring themselves to attend bluegrass concerts. They find the tuning peg halfway up the neck of a banjo profoundly upsetting, they write. It reminds them of a girl they knew in their childhood who had a sixth toe on her right foot. The author, possessing even then the thirst for knowledge that would later define their career in research, demanded to see it. They expected it to be among the gathering of toes atop the foot. Instead, it hung off the side, a limp, malformed nub.

Still another describes a feeling of displacement experienced at their home. They will reach out to flip a light switch where there is none. Walking upstairs, their foot will come down hard in expectation of a final step that is not there. There are other things too, other instances of banal surprise. What's more, they have lived in the house longer than they've lived anywhere aside from their childhood home, so it's not a matter of adjusting to the place. Nor is it some form of early-onset senility. They never got lost driving to work, for example. And in every place they've ever worked, including here at the Institute, everything is exactly where it should be, exactly where they expect. There's just something about their house, like the subtlest of hauntings. Despite their years there, they cannot get used to it, and thus can never feel fully at home. And yet, to sell the house and move would feel like letting the house win, something they cannot abide. "This place, terrible as it may often be, is a way of escaping without admitting defeat," the author writes in conclusion.

Elsewhere, there is speculation about other researchers. These notes are shorter, more concise: odors, personal hygiene deficiencies, suspected origins of a limp, potential couplings, the significance of a ring worn on the pointer finger, a thoughtless clicking noise someone makes with their tongue while working, a pretentious pronunciation of the word "ampere." As with the confessions, the authors do not sign these notes. Nor do they name their subjects, relying instead on vagaries such as "the tall one" or "the one with glasses" or, in one case that seems particularly mean, "the dog lady."

"Is this something they did for work?" Cline says. We've looked under all three tables in the room. All of them are covered, nearly corner to corner, with these handwritten messages.

"I don't think they'd have written on the bottom of the tables if it had to do with work," I say. "Also, it doesn't seem very professional."

"Good point," Cline says.

"But speaking of work, we need to keep moving." I get to my feet, thankful for this unexpected and amicable conclusion to our discussion of spin.

Cline also stands, and we gather our golf balls and make our way to the next room. On the way, Cline asks, "So, what was it then?"

"The writing under the tables?" I say. "I don't know. Perhaps it was a way to let off steam after long hours researching."

"No, I was talking about that," Cline says. "The research. Like, what did they actually do here? What did they study?"

"Oh," I say. "A wide variety of things."

"Right," Cline says. "That makes sense."

To be clear, my response is not exactly a lie, but a hypothesis based on the information available, that information being the size of the building and the number of rooms. There seems to be no way the researchers stationed here would be researching a limited number of things. Otherwise, the building would be smaller, or the rooms would be larger to accommodate more researchers working concurrently to gather the same data. Yet it remains a hypothesis, because the truth is I know just as little as Cline on this subject. And unlike other blind spots in my understanding of the Northern Institute, this one seems by design. While I'm not sure about the length of the helicopter ride or if Kay at some point mentioned the total number of rooms within the building, I'm certain the word "research" was not attached to a specific subject at any point of the onboarding. Furthermore, one of my most distinct recollections from our training is Kay pronouncing the word with the *-ch* as its own sharpened syllable, the same sound a lock makes as it's engaged, lending it a sense of unquestionable finality. Which is perhaps why, when I considered the consequences of an un-flat table assessed as flat, I pictured only the hazy outline of what the unlucky piece of equipment might be—something like a microscope, perhaps, or an apparatus for holding a test tube—and then a mess of gears, glass, and unidentifiable debris following its fall.

As we enter the next room, I try to bring this image into

focus, to actually imagine these rooms bustling with researchers and equipment, but again I see only the outlines of things: white lab coats, shining metal, something jotted onto a clipboard. These thoughts distract me as I set my golf ball down on a table, and I am not as careful as I've been when relinquishing my grip. Feeling the golf ball move, I overcorrect, which only sends it moving faster and farther. The noise of it rolling, quiet as it is, draws Cline's attention. The ball rolls in no peculiar pattern this time and comes to rest before he even turns to look.

"It's fine," I assure him.

But Cline has already made his way across the room. He gets down on the ground, sliding under the table on his back. "Just double-checking it."

"Yes," I say, following his lead, "due diligence."

17.

Each morning for the rest of the week, the three of us converge at my office. I arrive first, as always, to start the coffee. Next comes Cline, giddy and unencumbered. Finally, often mere minutes before nine, Gibbs hurries in, a cache of notebooks under her arms. When one of us asks how the work is going, she smiles and sighs, saying something vague, like "It's getting there" or "Oh, you know," despite the fact that our very separation dictates that we don't know. Eventually, we go our way, and she remains behind, unaware that the two of us have been on our own journey of discovery.

At first we act with deliberate clumsiness when putting down our golf balls, hoping for a roll that will give us an excuse to assess the tables' undersides, but this grows tiresome. As the week progresses, we simply walk into each room, quickly apply our golf balls, and then check under the tables without any pretense of structural inspection. We find nearly every one covered with handwritten text. After some time, we give up entirely on the autobiographical confessions, which meander and reveal very little about life at the Institute. We instead focus on the notes in which the author speculates about their fellow researchers.

Two threads arise. First, there is something about a rash. Its origins are not discussed, only its appearances:

Rash observed emerging from the shower. Appears to be growing, scabbing over.

And its texture:

Worked late with the rash yesterday evening. Gave a pat to the back under the guise of a job well done. Could feel it through the sweater. Despite protective layer washed hands vigorously.

And its hue:

Coloration of rash seems to shift with mood. Angry: eggplant. Sad: plum. Will continue experiments to see if color shifts for embarrassment and anxiety.

There are no names. Obviously we wouldn't recognize them if there were, but we find that without them we cannot tell how many are afflicted by the rash. It could have been one or two people, or it could have spread through the Institute, an infection that even the researchers could not explain.

More to our interest, though, are the notes about a figure

referred to only as "the hiker." The way Cline and I come to understand it is this: the hiker was one of the researchers, specifically one who did not suffer from the same snow sickness as the others. The notes, of course, are in no particular order, but Cline and I intuit a chronology: the hiker first discovered their unique resistance to the area's conditions after a fellow researcher dared them to spend twenty minutes outside. Over time, the duration of their stints out on the snow increased, as did the distance they traveled from the Northern Institute. One note claims to have seen them walk fifty yards out and back. In another note, a group of researchers went from room to room, window to window, watching as the hiker hiked the entire perimeter of the building. Finally, there were some rumors of the hiker planning to construct a camp, but we cannot find any discussion concerning their success or failure in doing this.

"Do you think that's what the thing in the snow is?" Cline asks, as we move between rooms on the fourth floor. "The hiker's camp?"

"It's very possible," I say, and it's true: this is perhaps the most logical theory about the thing in the snow put forward yet. Still, I don't like the idea of mining the undersides of the tables for clues about our current situation. It feels reductive, and if anything, I've enjoyed the escape from the tense dynamic that dominated our workflow last week. For this reason, when Cline asks, "Should we show Gibbs any of this? In case it might help her write the description?" I shake my head.

"I think she has all she needs," I say. "I would hate for any of this to make her second-guess herself."

"What about Gilroy?" Cline asks. "Could we ask him?"

The answer to this question turns out to be no. We cannot ask Gilroy because we do not see him. Or, we see him, but only from a distance. He seems to be forever rounding a corner or slipping into a room, ignoring us when we call to him, and disappearing before we arrive where we had seen him. Instead, we find pages of frantic writing he's left behind. One reads:

All attempts to battle the cold through apparel ultimately fail. Cold-weather wear that is designed to breathe lets the cold in, but worse are those items that allow no such entry. They keep our warmth so close that our body eventually perspires to cool itself, but when we remove the item out of discomfort the cold finds an easily won ally in our sweat-soaked forms, evidence that the cold does not just want us, but we want the cold, that our beings are seeking to hasten the slow march toward their eventual end.

Another:

Consider the act of ice fishing. A man dons his warmest garments, assembles a tent upon a frozen lake, cuts a hole in the surface of the water turned solid by the rapidly dipping temperature, and lowers his line. In other words, he makes himself impervious to the cold in order to hunt a creature that is naturally so. Is this for the sport of it? Or does he feel the need to make himself the enemy of the fish simply because the fish does not share an enemy of his?

And another:

That the cold attacks, disproportionately, one's manhood is not merely a matter of biology; it is symbolic of the cold's end goal, a full-blown castration of the soul.

Some trail off midsentence. Others possess only two or three words. Many cover the front and back of each page with thoughts that are, to me, entirely inscrutable, contrasting with the clarity and concision of the notes under the table. Cline shows no interest in reading these screeds. He simply hands them to me when he finds them and says, "Another Gilroy thing." I collect them and return them to my office at the end of each day, where Gibbs, finishing up her work for the day, doesn't even ask what they are as I deposit them into a desk drawer.

I find myself once again alone with the mystery of Gilroy.

18.

Our pace picks up near the end of the week, the table density thinning with each subsequent floor. There are more desks, it seems, the higher we go, but none of these contain the graffiti that has captured our interest. We should have no problem finishing on time, but Friday morning I lose count of how many scoops of coffee I've added to the machine. The result is a highly potent brew and shaky hands that send golf balls rolling every which way. Luckily Cline agrees to press on until we are finished.

When, at long last, I return to my office, it's almost six, and I am surprised to find Gibbs still at work herself.

"It's the end of the day already?" Gibbs says.

"We actually went a bit over," I say.

She looks over her shoulder, out the window into the dim light of dusk. "Huh."

I'd like to metabolize this scene into something I can smirk at: the entire week at her disposal and here I find her, pushing right up to the final minute. But I can't. The pages of the notebooks spread out in front of her are full—upside down, I can read words scrawled in all caps across the top of one page: "UPPER PROTRUSION: 'CONICAL' OR 'FUNNEL-LIKE'???"—and her eyes appear heavy with exhaustion, not wide with the stress of procrastination.

"The paperwork won't take long," I say. "I can come back in an hour, if you need more time."

Gibbs looks down at the page in front of her as if she is examining an open wound. "No. No, I should just finish it." She takes a deep breath and writes, bringing the text to the very edge of the very bottom corner of the page. She pauses a moment, adds a period, and then pushes the chair back and stands. "Okay, done."

While she gathers her materials, I move to the chair. "Just this page then?" I ask.

Gibbs looks at me in way that indicates I've asked the wrong question.

"Not that it has to be more than a page," I say.

"It's all there. Or most of it. There's plenty. Enough, at least."

"Great." And because it seems rude to begin the paperwork while she's still collecting her things, I say: "Do you feel good about it?"

Gibbs, hastily closing all her notebooks, pauses. "Do I feel good about what?"

I hold up the description.

"Oh," she says. "Yeah, totally. I mean, it is what it is. I got it. Or as much as I could. Which, I mean, it's enough. Or, it's good. I think it's good. It was a lot. But not too much. Just a lot, though." She seems woozy on her feet.

"The helicopter won't be here for several hours," I say. "I could read it, if you want some feedback."

"No." She sounds like the thought makes her sick. "No, that's all right. It's fine. It's ready to go."

"Okay, sounds good," I say.

We stand there a moment, neither of us talking, Gibbs's eyes locked on the description in front of me, her expression like someone under hypnosis.

"Well," I say, slowly and loudly, "have a nice weekend."

Gibbs blinks hard and meets my eyes. "Yes," she says. "It's the weekend." She moves to leave, but turns back when she reaches the doorway. "You too. A nice weekend." Then she's gone, leaving me alone in the office.

I fill in the blank on the paperwork with a zero and write out a quick Post-it.

> *Kay*—
> *You will find, herewith, the additional information you requested with regard to the thing we have seen in the snow. Please let me know if you require any further clarification.*
> *Best,*
> *Hart*

I am not sure if this is entirely necessary. Gibbs's description will likely make its purpose known. Still, with all the frustrations the thing in the snow has caused, it seems best to be overcautious in ensuring the message is received. I certainly do not write the Post-it out of jealousy of Gibbs's opportunity to communicate directly with Kay. Nor is it an attempt to take ownership of a description very clearly composed in someone else's hand. At least I tell myself as much.

With the Post-it adhered, I place Gibbs's description atop the paperwork in the folder. I don't plan to read it, but certain phrases jump out at me. She describes the base ("of what we can see") as a "stony pillow" that "expands to a narrow soft tip," the entire thing possessing "a subdued glossy matte shine." With each thing that catches my eye, I feel my own experience of the thing in the snow—the long, strange moment I spent looking at it as I made my ill-conceived leap to the stage last week— clarify in front of me.

It's perfect.

This realization and my aggressive closing of the folder oc- cur so rapidly, I can't be sure which follows which. I should go to the roof, I should deposit the paperwork and the descrip- tion, and I should commence my weekend. But I don't. In- stead, I look for my description of the lamp, finding it with the others—the winning entry and the disqualifying drawing— stashed in a desk drawer, by Gibbs, I assume.

Cline had described it as "clinical," which seemed dispar- aging at the time, but reading it over again, I see it's the most generous word one could apply to my work. "Childish" or "sim- ple" would be more apt, the writing of a man who seeks only to convey whatever detail his eye happens upon next, with no concern for cohesion or ease of understanding. I read sentence after rote, uninspired sentence until finally I come to a black square, something crossed out. I forget the cause of this until the vague shapes of an *m* and a *p* present themselves from beneath the scribble. In defiance of the rules, I'd unthinkingly written the word "lamp" before seeking to rectify the mistake.

I close my eyes to bring the reading exercise to an end, but when I do, a thought comes to me, crystal clear: Gibbs is destined for greater things than I am. Maybe she's already arrived. Gibbs has spent a week depleting herself in the pursuit of clarity, whereas I have been traipsing through the Institute with Cline, allowing rushed work so that we may indulge in the under-table gossip of a group of people we will never meet. All the details of this past week point to my being leapfrogged.

A shock of pain pulses through my face, the base of every hair in my beard tingling with hurt simultaneously, before falling into a pattern. I open my eyes again and find the room almost entirely dark. Night had barely begun to fall when I'd closed them, seemingly only moments ago, but suddenly I'm standing in darkness, pondering this pronounced, unmistakable discomfort. How long have I been standing here, I wonder as I move to turn on the overhead light. With no daylight to battle, its Morse-like flicker cannot be denied. It falls perfectly in line with the throb of my beard.

I hear something outside, a strange slicing sound, and my attention snaps to the window.

Outside, the thing in the snow glows.

How it glows I cannot say. The moonlight can barely make it through the cloud cover here, so it can't be reflecting that, not so brightly at least. And besides, the glow seems to shift and brighten and cast out across the icy white sheet surrounding it. It's as if it's awakening and surveying its domain.

It's coming alive, I think. It's coming for us.

It takes another moment for me to look up and see the light moving through the sky above.

Of course. The helicopter. That explains the chopping noise as well, and a rush of relief overwhelms me, followed almost immediately by terror. I haven't deposited the week's paperwork in the lockbox.

There's no time for my ritual of looking over the snow sickness symptom card. I grab the folder off my desk and I run. By the time I reach the roof, I can hear the helicopter just outside. It has not yet landed. Bursting out of the door, my entire body nearly seizes up. My legs cry out in pain, my arms too. I try to breathe, but the air feels almost solid. I did not have time to stop at my quarters for my more insulated clothing, and I've never experienced just how cold it is in only a sweater and a pair of flannel-lined work pants.

The helicopter hovers overhead, making its descent. I stagger to the lockbox, deposit the file, and then make my way back inside, hearing its wheels touch down the moment after the door clicks shut behind me.

I lean against the wall, filling my lungs as the helicopter's engine slowly comes to rest. The Northern Institute has never felt as warm as it does now, but I cannot stop shivering. My pulse pounds in my ears, which is likely why I don't hear the footsteps. The door swings open into me just as I've managed to get control of myself.

I scream and the woman screams too.

"Jesus, are you hiding?" she shouts. "Are you trying to scare the crap out of me? What kind of welcome is this?" She lets the door close behind her, but huddles at the far end of the small vestibule. She carries two large duffel bags, one over each shoulder.

"I was just depositing the week's paperwork," I say, before the obvious question occurs to me: "I'm sorry, but who are you?"

The woman squints at me in the light of the single bulb hanging above us. It blinks just slightly in a pattern that does not seem to repeat. After what feels like an interminably long pause, during which I fight the urge to look up, she answers: "I'm the health specialist. You didn't forget about my visit, did you?"

"No," I say. "Of course not."

19.

I had entirely forgotten about the health specialist's visit, so the weekend proceeds in a way unlike any other since our arrival.

We have no medical benefits, as medical benefits would be of little benefit to us all the way out here. If there is a medical emergency, we are to send a message to Kay via the button next to the door on the roof. There are a series of codes, conveying everything from "separated appendage" to "mild but persistent discomfort of the teeth." Kay assures us that, in cases such as these, the helicopter will be dispatched, we will be taken from the Northern Institute, and the medical procedure will be "taken care of," after which we will be returned to our post, if such a thing is possible.

But for general checkups, the health specialist comes every six months. This is her first visit. When Kay told us about her during our onboarding, Gibbs asked what kind of health she would be checking. "All aspects of health," Kay replied, explaining that the health specialist is a pan-wellness practitioner, one capable of measuring both mental and physical health and administering solutions for ailments in either sphere. "She will also give haircuts," Kay told us.

From this framing, I've always imagined the health specialist to be another Kay, a beacon of efficiency, someone who understands our way of life even if she does not currently live it. This characterization proves entirely inaccurate.

"Is there a room ready for me?" she asks.

Of course there isn't, so I take her to one of the empty suites, lying that I'd wanted to give her the option of choosing a room herself. She seems indifferent to this.

I fetch some spare bedding from a nearby supply closet and return to find her sitting on the bed, peering around the room.

"Where's the thermostat?" she asks.

"The thermostat?"

"Yes," she says, once again looking around the room. "To turn up the heat in here. I was really hoping you'd be more ready for me. It could take an hour to warm this room up."

"There is no thermostat in here," I say.

"Is there one for the suite?" she asks.

"There's only one thermostat for the whole Institute," I say.

"Where's that one?" the health specialist asks.

"I don't know," I say. "Kay has it set to the optimal temperature."

"*This* is the optimal temperature?" the health specialist says. "It's always this cold here?"

"The blankets are very warm," I say.

"I hope so," she says.

She comes to my room in the morning.

"I knocked on all the doors in this suite," she says. "I hope I didn't wake anyone."

"There's only one of us in each suite," I say. I'm thankful I'd been up long enough to dress.

"Well, what's the plan?" she says. "When can we start?"

"Start," I say.

"The health checks," says the health specialist.

"It's the weekend," I say. "The others are off."

"Can you gather them?" the health specialist says. She stands in the threshold of my quarters and I realize that I have been the only person in this room for the entirety of our stay at the Institute. I have given no thought to its cleanliness or lack thereof, because it is essentially a cocoon. You don't need to worry about others scrutinizing the inside of your shoes, and you don't need to worry about others scrutinizing the inside of your quarters. A quick glance around reveals nothing to be concerned about, which is itself a thing of some concern. The Leader books line a small shelf next to the desk—its surface clear, just like the walls—that sits beneath the single small porthole window. The ruffled blankets on my bed, the electric kettle letting off a light steam, my tea-stained mug—these provide the only evidence that a living being occupies this space. I should have a rug, or some art, but I've never considered it until now.

"Why would I gather them?" I ask.

"So we can begin the health checks."

"I thought we would start on Monday," I tell her.

Her eyes narrow and her face takes on an expression of disgust. "Then why am I here now?"

"The helicopter runs only on Friday nights," I say. "Except in case of an emergency."

"So even if we started immediately," the health specialist says, "I still couldn't leave until Friday night?"

"That's correct," I say.

The health specialist shakes her head. "So I just sit in my room, for two days?"

"You can move about the Institute," I tell her.

Though my suggestion is not met with enthusiasm, the health specialist does take it to heart. She certainly moves about the Institute, specifically the stretch of the Institute between her room and mine. She wants to know first if there is some sort of lounge with comfortable couches. There is not. Then she wants to know if there is a gym, with treadmills and weights. There is not. Later, she comes back and wants to know "what the deal is" with the "fresh-juice situation." This alarms me at first, as it sounds like something I will be called on to deal with, but upon further interrogation, I find that the situation with the fresh juice is that there is no fresh juice.

"What *do* you have here?" she finally asks.

All this time at the Northern Institute, we have been busy confirming what we have: a number of stable chairs; predominantly level surfaces that hold up to multi-point golf ball scrutiny; doors whose volume does not exceed what is natural, as established by a diverse committee of listeners, likely with a variety of different door volume expectations. In other words, we have many things. But to listen to the health specialist, you'd think the entire building was empty.

It would be an interesting meditation on perspective if it weren't so annoying.

The health specialist's many visits impede upon my level of comfort. Concerned with appearing worthy of my leadership role, I do not spend as many hours lounging in bed as I usually do. I sit at the small desk, reading book eleven of the Leader series (*A Most Motley Crew*). This more dignified position irreparably alters the chemistry of the weekend.

Previously, I could enjoy the chronology of a narrative even while time contorted itself in strange ways around me, scrambling my sense of general order. This weekend, the seconds march neatly by in order, one after the other, each one presenting itself with sickening clarity. The pages in front of me, meanwhile, feel like a riddle I cannot solve. When Jack French finds himself in the rear of a crew boat, clutching an ornate vase printed all over with Arabic letters under one arm and the few pages of notes for his essential treatise on management under the other, calling out orders to the team of amateur rowers—attendees of some sort of conference on medical illustration, each one jealous of the others for reasons I cannot discern—I do not know how they ended up there, nor do I understand the vase's significance or, in turn, why they are being pursued by a group of men in masks made to look like various livestock. Several times I think to check the description on the back of the book, but this feels like a failure of reading.

The reason for my lack of concentration is twofold. First, I find myself listening deeply to the ambient noise of the building, attempting to discern the sounds of approaching footsteps from the room's low buzz, indicating the health specialist's return with another unfulfillable request. This, unfortunately, leads me to look for patterns in said buzz, and mapping those patterns onto the low throb at the base of my beard.

Second, I cannot concentrate due to the cold, which I feel more acutely than ever. Without the warmth of my blanket, nor the heat of movement that accompanies even our most basic weekly tasks, I cannot get comfortable. This seems like something that Kay's team failed to take into account when setting the optimal temperature for fiscal conservancy without sacrificing productivity: stillness. I consider putting on my outside apparel, but given that the entire reason for sitting at the desk is not to appear ridiculous, and given that the health specialist's initial complaint concerned the temperature, I think it best to remain in my sweater and my fleece-lined pants, to create the illusion that comfort is possible here even as it eludes me. I do, however, wear my boots and my wool socks, and continually refill my mug with coffee and hot tea. Each sip provides only momentary reprieve. A feeling of stiffness pervades everything, so that when I turn the pages of my book, the various ligaments in my knuckles respond to their commands slowly and with a mild ache.

I wonder if this indicates some flaw of Gilroy's research, that perhaps this sort of cold could be worse than the extreme cold he seeks to explore. After all, the depths of cold into which he regularly sends his figurative charges are characterized by an end point of release: numbness, fatigue, and death. The cold I experience in my room, trying and failing to read the next book in the Leader series, registers as a slight yet persistent pain, an unending purgatory of misery that refuses to put me out of itself.

Once or twice, I escape my quarters to do some laps, not bothering to tell the health specialist where I'm going, so that I might be alone with my thoughts, but she manages to intrude upon these as well. My mind draws up a scene of her knocking on my door and walking off in a huff after finding me gone, an image that fills me with a mix of anxiety and frustration. Otherwise, I find myself rehashing our initial meeting in the vestibule, imagining ways I might have handled things with more composure, to start things off on a better foot and potentially undercut her disappointment with the Institute. But it's difficult to picture this meeting without some sense of shock.

While it concerns me that her arrival came as such a

surprise, this can be explained: her role and the frequency of her visits were just two data points among many during our hasty onboarding. What is more troubling is what else I might have missed in the intervening time—given the unchanging nature of this place, inside and out, we've long since lost track of everything but the days of the workweek.

When we first arrived here, I put up a calendar in my office, each page displaying the photograph of a cornucopia appropriate to that month. The effect was jarring, the brightness of the images on the wall competing with the static view from the office window. Soon enough, I forgot to turn the page and lost track of where we were, opting to use the tasks as measurements of time in lieu of months and seasons. For this reason—and also because Cline mentioned there being some "significant cornucopia-related backlash" in "certain corners of the art world"—I eventually took the calendar down. The others did not protest. They didn't even seem to notice.

I wish now I had not discarded it but kept it somewhere, in my desk or my quarters. It might help me remember when exactly we started, which could then help me determine the current month and day. With these two dates, I could assess if there were any significant events I have overlooked. Have we missed Christmas, for example? I cannot imagine Cline or Gibbs allowing such heartlessness as being forced to work through a major holiday to go unaddressed, even if it weren't intentional. But what if they, too, have lost track of the date? This thought relieves me of only some of my guilt. I am the team's supervisor. I should be the one with the answers in cases such as these.

I take some time back in my room laying out the twelve potential six-month stretches we may have just completed, listing as best as I can from memory the holidays that occur in each one. There are some six-month periods in which few notable holidays fall, and I hope that we've been living in one of these. But I have another fear: that the health specialist will conduct her week of health checks, leave, and return in six months with Cline, Gibbs, and me having celebrated nothing.

When the night finally arrives, I welcome it, and not just because it is an opportunity to finally climb under my covers and experience the only true warmth at the Northern Institute. The week will be strange, but the sooner Monday arrives, the sooner we will get through it and resume some semblance of normalcy.

Only as I am nodding off do I realize that this is just the first night in the weekend, Saturday, and I have another unstructured day to contend with tomorrow.

Sunday goes much the same way. It feels interminably long, the minutes in front of me like a trail of diamonds stretching infinitely across the floor, each one as clear and jagged as it is dense and impenetrable. It is the opposite of a typical weekend at the Northern Institute. Rather than absolute solitude, I experience a heightened sense of awareness, but this only leads me to a higher plane of disorientation with each passing minute. I close my book and cannot recall what I just read. I go to top off my tea mug with hot water, and it spills out onto the desk, already filled to the brim. I walk to the first floor to do more laps, but return after just one, stopping on the third floor to sit behind the desk in my office, a detour whose purpose I do not know.

Eventually, night comes again, but as I attempt to sleep, part of me fears that I will awake to another Sunday somehow, that this terrible weekend will continue indefinitely into the future. The fear keeps me awake well into the night. It's late, but I don't care: I pour myself a glass of fortified wine, a reward for getting through the weekend this time. My eyelids grow heavy with the first sip, and just as I finish it, sleep finally arrives.

In this way, another weekend at the Northern Institute passes.

20.

On Monday morning, I don't bother checking the assignment folder lockbox or the supplies hutch. I simply unload the provisions and then make my way to the office to start the coffee.

"No folder?" Gibbs says when she and Cline arrive.

"There's no assignment this week," I say. "The health specialist is here."

"The wealth specialist?" Cline said. "Like a financial planner?"

"Health," Gibbs says, enunciating, "not wealth."

"Oh," Cline says. "Well, that's better. I'm not a fan of consumerism. Health is good, though."

"So it's been six months already?" Gibbs says.

"Hard to believe, isn't it?" I say.

"When does she arrive?" Cline asks.

"I'm already here," comes a voice from the doorway.

We turn and find the health specialist waiting. She has a bag hoisted over her shoulder and, for some reason, looks exhausted. Perhaps it took something out of her, exhausting me with her demands and umbrage at their un-meet-ability. Her presence registers like indigestion: a discomfort I work to keep invisible. It's not just the difficulty she's caused me since her arrival. The mere fact of a fourth person in the office is enough to throw the entire dynamic of the room off balance.

"I've been here all weekend, actually, for reasons that I don't totally understand," she says, stepping fully into the room. Gibbs, to make way for her, shifts her position, situating herself at the window, easily the coldest place in the entire room. Why she would do this—why anyone would willingly rest their back against a window in the Institute—confounds me. To add to this confusion, I realize she has precisely oriented herself to block anyone's view of the thing in the snow.

Seeing the coffee machine, the health specialist lets out a sigh of relief. "Oh thank god. I'll take a cup."

I exchange a look with the other two.

"We have only three mugs," I say.

The health specialist blinks a long, pained blink. "What?"

"There are only the three of us who meet for coffee each morning," I say. "So we keep only three mugs in the office. But we have plenty of coffee, and we did provide you with a mug in your room, if you wanted to retrieve that—"

"What floor is this?" the health specialist says, cutting me off.

"The third," I say.

"And what floor is my room on?" asks the health specialist.

"The sixth," I say.

The math does not justify the abhorrence that flashes across her face. She opens her mouth to unleash, I would assume, a

123

tirade expressing her cumulative lack of enthusiasm for this place and, because I am its chief representative, me. But before she can say a word, Gibbs holds out her mug, her back barely relinquishing the window. "Have mine," she says. "I haven't even taken a sip yet."

This gesture of kindness throws the health specialist. She cannot help but smile warmly at Gibbs. "Oh, I couldn't."

"Really," Gibbs says, "I've been trying to cut down."

"Are you sure?" the health specialist ventures, and Gibbs nods her consent. The health specialist takes a generous drink of coffee and her eyes moisten, as if she's on the verge of tears. "Thank you," she says to Gibbs. Then, to the rest of us: "I usually begin with a short discussion of the relativity of health. We could stay here, but it's a bit tight."

"There's a nice conference room across the floor," Gibbs offers.

"With flat tables," Cline adds, "and stable chairs."

The health specialist stares at him for a time, before turning to Gibbs. "That sounds great. Lead the way."

Gibbs's swift snatching of the reins confirms the fears I felt last Friday, standing in my office, looking at her description of the thing in the snow without reading it. But I can muster neither resentment nor despair, only befuddlement: first with her behavior in the office, and now with her decision to lead us all the way to the other side of the third floor, where the windows will look out upon nothing.

When we arrive at the conference room she's chosen—one that is no different from any other room, really—the health specialist places her coffee down at the head of the table and removes the bag from her shoulder. "I'll need the shades drawn," she says. "Oh, and where's the projector?"

"There is no projector," I say.

Again, she looks at me in a way that conveys a lesser form of hatred, reserved for situations when full-blown hatred would be a waste. "Three mugs in the office and no projector in the conference room," she mutters to herself. "This should make the presentation interesting."

"If you have materials," Gibbs says, "we could pass them around."

The health specialist shakes her head. "That won't work. They're slides, so they're very small, and we haven't done the eye exam yet. No, I guess I'll just run through the presentation and describe the visuals as best I can. I've done it enough. I know them by heart at this point. We haven't done the hearing test yet either, but I'll just try and speak loudly. Does that sound okay?"

Cline, Gibbs, and I mumble in the affirmative.

"Great." The health specialist hangs her bag on the shoulder of a nearby chair, takes a swig of her coffee, and begins, suddenly speaking with an uncanny level of polish. "Welcome, all, to a week of wellness checks. As your MediScope representative, I'm excited to lead you on this journey toward measuring and understanding your personal health, as well as setting goals for a healthier future. Now, so I know where to start, can I see, by a show of hands, how many of you have been through a MediScope wellness week before?"

None of us raise our hands.

"I'm sorry," I say. "What is MediScope?"

"MediScope is the company I work for," the health specialist says.

"You mean you don't work with Kay?" I ask.

"MediScope is a mobile health solutions company that works in service of geographically diverse workforces," the health specialist says. When none of us reacts to this, she elaborates. "Basically, companies with remotely located employees contract with us, and we follow best-in-class practices to administer clear and concise health checks on-site, so as not to interrupt workflow."

"Huh," I say.

"Anyway, it's no problem that you're all new," says the health specialist. "We can start from the beginning. MediScope isn't just a name. It's a guiding philosophy. We administer a wide scope of health checks to a wide scope of people."

"Oh," Cline says, "'scope.' I thought you said 'soap' at first, like it was a product, a healing soap or something."

The health specialist ignores this. "But we also believe that health itself is a range, not a singularly defined quality." She pauses and takes another drink from her coffee. "At this point, there should be a slide showing a sort of stick figure character rubbing its head, standing next to a shelf in a cupboard. On the various shelves are food items. To the character's right is a ruler." The health specialist clears her throat and resumes her rehearsed tone. "Consider this man. There are certain things that are accessible to him, given his height, and other things that are not, such as those things on the top shelf."

"What's on the top shelf?" Cline asks.

"Just various items," the health specialist says.

"I'm someone who really needs specifics," Cline says, "when it comes to hypotheticals."

"Fine," the health specialist says. "Let's say flour. And potatoes. Something like that. Just typical things you'd find in a pantry."

"Well, I hope this guy didn't want to make any bread," Cline says. "Or gnocchi."

"Cline," I say.

"Just seems like an organizational flaw," Cline says, addressing this to me for some reason, "to put essentials all the way up there. Like, flour and potatoes? They'd be right in the middle for me. The top would be where I stash stuff I use infrequently. Say, a shelf-stable paste for making a spicy foreign soup." He turns back to the health specialist. "Not that I don't endorse a varied diet."

"I think this is all just a metaphor," Gibbs says.

"Exactly," the health specialist says. "I usually wouldn't comment on the food items. They're just little pictures used to help illustrate something."

"Just little pictures," Cline mumbles under his breath, sitting back, clearly insulted. "Wow. Would hate for the artist to hear that."

"All I mean to say," says the health specialist, "is that health is relative. Just like the man can't reach all of the things on the shelves, not everyone can reach certain levels of health, and we shouldn't feel bad, or make others feel bad, about that."

"How would it even be possible to make each other feel bad?" I say. "Our health records will be confidential, right?"

"Of course your records will be kept confidential," the health specialist says. "But some of the activities will be completed as a group. Which brings me to our next slide. Here would usually be a screen showing what the week will entail. Now, your employer opted for the basic package. That means: a basic blood pressure check, a basic reflexes check, a basic weight check, a basic eye exam, a basic ear exam, a basic coordination test, a basic stress test, a basic mental health examination, a basic dental exam and teeth cleaning, a number of basic stretching and fitness exercises, et cetera."

"Aren't there supposed to be haircuts?" Cline whispers to Gibbs.

"Haircuts might be in the 'et cetera,'" Gibbs offers.

"That's exactly where the basic haircuts are, yes," says the health specialist.

"How will it break down," I say, "in terms of which will be completed in a group, and which will be completed individually?"

"I can't tell you that," says the health specialist.

"You can't?" I say.

"MediScope believes that an extremely limited disclosure of the week's schedule and structure will lead to the extraction of more honest, organic personal data," says the health specialist.

"What you're saying is, we can't know what's going to happen when," I say, "or how it will happen?"

"That's correct," says the health specialist.

"So we can't prepare," I say.

"Exactly," says the health specialist. "And while your employer did not select MediScope's premium or platinum packages, I am certified, as well as equipped, to carry out any of the procedures featured in them, the cost of which, Kay tells me, can be deducted from your stipends. And these can be scheduled."

"We don't know what the premium or platinum procedures are," I say.

"Those are probably on the slide," Gibbs says.

"Yes," the health specialist says, "they are. And I'd list them, but frankly there are too many. A full joint analysis, hair dyeing, hot stone massage, that sort of thing. Although, around here, it would likely be a lukewarm stone massage." She laughs at her own joke and Gibbs laughs with her. "Really, if there's anything you need taken care of, health-wise, just ask and I'll let you know if it's a basic, premium, or platinum health procedure."

"Earwax," Cline says.

"What was that?" the health specialist says.

"Had a bit of an ear thing this weekend," Cline says, "so I used the thing that you're not supposed to use, but that everyone uses. Except that just made it worse, which I guess is why they say not to use it. Now I'm working with one ear, which is fine, because it's my good ear, and besides, I'm more of a visual learner, which has made this session a bit tough for me, but I think I get the gist. Anyway, I think it would be good to get the wax out."

The room is silent for a moment, aside from the codelike buzz of the lights.

"We can deal with that once we get to the ear exam," the health specialist says. "Depending on the extent of the clog, it might be covered under the basic package. But, if it's very severe, it might be a premium procedure. Or even platinum. That's not likely, but I've seen things in this job you wouldn't believe."

She looks at Gibbs as she says this, and Gibbs nods in a knowing way. It occurs to me that if anyone should be enjoying this sort of camaraderie, it should be me: looks exchanged between two people in positions of authority. But I am left to listen un-glanced-upon as the presentation continues. Some of the unseen slides involve a number of images clearly related to health. There are hearts in both medical and simplified renderings, medicine bottles, that sort of thing. Others seem less on topic. The health specialist describes a jungle scene, a rowboat, a peeled anthropomorphic onion frowning and teary-eyed as it wallows in its own stink. Without visuals, the through line is hard to follow, and I quickly lose it.

Finally it comes to an end with the health specialist saying, "And that's what makes better health better health. Any questions?"

Gibbs shakes her head with purpose. Cline stares at the table in front of him, as if asleep with his eyes open. I check the clock on the wall and stand.

"Thank you for that," I say. "An excellent overview. Shall we eat lunch and reconvene for another session after that?"

The health specialist glares at me as if amazed at how someone can be so wrong so often. "That's all we cover on day one," she says.

And with that, we are released into a wilderness of free time.

21.

Without the schedule presented to us beforehand, the week becomes a terror. Each day, we meet in my office. Each day, we proceed from there to another corner of the third floor, where, either privately or as a group, we go through a series of health checks. Each day, I worry that not only will the agenda call for a weigh-in, but that it will be done with all of us together in the same room. When the day's session finally reaches its end just before the lunch hour, I stalk up to the kitchen on the sixth floor, gather my provisions, and bring them to my quarters, where I eat, nibbling lightly at first, as if I might trick a scale with just a few days of willpower. Ultimately, I realize the futility of this and eat the rest of my meal with a ravenousness achievable only through self-loathing.

It's not just the potential presence of the others witnessing my embarrassment. It's the end of my freedom from the mathematical exactitude of my body being assigned a number. The last time I stepped on a scale was before our arrival here.

I cannot remember exactly what it said, and even if I could, it wouldn't matter. That was a different time, another life. I was free of that number as soon as we stepped from the helicopter. Our way of life at the Institute changed many aspects of me: the way I must act as a supervisor, the way I must dress to combat the cold, the way I sleep, the way I eat, the amount I move in a given day. I know my body is different than it was when I arrived, and that is all I need to know, not if it's bigger or smaller or more muscular or any of that. So what I fear most is a number, as a number will lock me into the me that exists here.

The only benefit of the looming weigh-in is that my concerns about it insulate me from other concerns. As we move through a series of calisthenics, for example, and I am the only one who cannot touch my toes while sitting with my feet straight out in front of me—a stretch that has haunted me my entire life, and whose function I cannot understand, given that humans have evolved to possess a hinge known as the knee at their leg's center—I do not feel shame, so great is my dread of the potential for greater shame in the near future. Likewise, Gibbs's temporary usurpation of my role, which would usually fill me with ire, leaves me numb, and, if I'm completely honest, thankful; were I required to remain the group's leader in the face of such a threat to my ego as a public weighing, I doubt I could make it through the days at all.

Furthermore, said usurpation comes with a nice side effect: her outright refusal to discuss or look at (or let anyone else discuss or look at) the thing in the snow. In the mornings, she continues to stand with her back to it, blocking it, and when the health specialist asks for a room in which to carry out the day's events, Gibbs sends us to the opposite side of the building. I cannot seem to trace the origin of this shift. One theory would be that the week she spent alone with it has exhausted her interest in it. But that doesn't explain why it's so important that none of us be able to look at it. So I settle upon a second theory: that Gibbs, by taking on the important job of describing the thing in the snow, finally experienced a modicum of true authority, which naturally led her to understand the disruption that the thing in the snow poses. I'd be proud of her, had I the capacity to feel anything beyond worry.

Throughout the week, the health specialist, intentionally or not, makes clear the limitations of the "basic" plan Kay has selected for us. Her dental tools are made from a dense plastic that bends, rather than steel (premium) or titanium (platinum). Her eye chart features only five letters in various patterns. (The premium, she assures us, features fifteen, and the platinum, the entire alphabet.) The thermometer's readings come only in multiples of three, but we have the option to upgrade to the premium option of whole numbers or the platinum level, which includes decimals. As for the stethoscope, the health package in question determines the length of the tubing, which seems odd, as it impacts the health specialist more than us. Although, I will admit, this is when I most seriously consider upgrading, given the awkwardness of her leaning uncomfortably close to listen to my heart through the short tube, just barely over six inches long.

Each day's proceedings follow no logic I can understand. The various components of a traditional physical occur here and there throughout the week, arranged around lessons and round-table discussions about topics such as nutrition, happiness, digestion, and eyestrain. And while we finish early each day, the extra hours do nothing to help me discern when the weigh-in will land.

It finally arrives on Thursday, along with a blood pressure and stress level assessment, and of course it will be conducted privately (those words—"of course"—being the health specialist's, delivered with a slight grin, in response to my question about the format, as if I should have known as much, as if this week has been anything but an exercise in planned confusion). Still, the weight check has taken on such significance that this news brings no relief but rather a surge of jitters. My heart rate rises, sending the buzz of my beard into a tizzy.

We sit on chairs we've pulled into the hallway outside a room Gibbs has chosen, a former lab opposite the thing in the snow, that we call "the Coliseum" for reasons I no longer recall. I let the other two go first, hoping it will buy me some time to calm down, but in what feels like minutes, Cline and Gibbs are done and dispatched for the day.

"All right, you're up," the health specialist says, and it's as if she's speaking directly to my anxiety.

She holds the door open, and I walk in purposefully, eager to hide my apprehension. Without pause, I locate the scale in the corner of the room and stride directly to it, stopping inches away to loosen my boots' laces.

"We'll start with the stress assessment, actually," the health specialist says.

"Would it be possible to do the weigh-in first?" I ask. "I think otherwise my stress assessment might go poorly."

The health specialist studies me for a moment, confused. "Okay, fine," she says. "Stand up straight." She takes a measuring tape and checks my height, which is odd, but I don't question it. Next, she kneels down next to the scale to key something in. I return to my boots, but she says, "You can leave those on," and then gestures for me to step up.

"What about my sweater?" I say.

The health specialist shakes her head. "Too cold."

"I don't mind," I say.

"Really, it's not necessary," the health specialist says.

"Won't it affect the reading?" I ask.

"Not enough to worry about," she says.

Begrudgingly, I step onto the scale in my boots and heavy clothing, knowing full well that I will be greeted with a number I don't like. Except I'm not. After a few moments, the scale flashes "OVR."

The health specialist stands next to me with a clipboard. When she sees this, she makes a note with her pen. "Okay, great. Let's move on to the stress assessment."

I don't step off the scale. "But it's giving an error message."

"That's not an error message," the health specialist says.

"Then what is it?"

"The basic package only allows that I put the scale in 'basic' mode," the health specialist says. "I key in your height and then it flashes a code that corresponds to a basic weight assessment. Really, we're looking for extreme fluctuations here. The actual number doesn't matter."

"What height did you put in?" I ask.

"Seventy-four inches," the health specialist says.

"Which is, in feet?" I say.

"About six foot two," she says.

"I'm six foot four," I say.

"It wouldn't make that much of a difference," says the health specialist.

"And OVR stands for 'overweight'?"

"Correct," the health specialist says.

She does not speak with glee, nor does she hesitate or show a hint of empathy. As she sees it, she is merely speaking a fact: according to this scale—indeed, according to MediScope's basic package—I am overweight. And yes, there's an unkindness to the word. And yes, there is, in the back of my mind, a process starting up, running calculations to make the scale read something different when I next step on it six months from now. But without any concrete statistics, this urge will be short-lived. I have dreaded this weigh-in the way one might dread dental surgery, but there has been nothing surgical about it. Nothing has been taken away, nothing fixed in place, no procedure conducted with precision or expertise.

I am thankful for this, as I am thankful for the health specialist's rushed assessment of my height and insistence I leave my boots and sweater on, and I feel the need to express as much.

"Thank you," I tell the health specialist.

This takes her by surprise. She eyes me suspiciously, like I'm being sarcastic. "For what?"

"Just," I say, "this." I motion to the scale.

She looks at the reading again, scrutinizing it, as if to see something she'd missed. After a moment, she says, "Sure, yeah," and then begins to prepare for the stress assessment.

22.

The day has gone better than I had hoped, but a week of such intense stress (I'd heard the health specialist mumble "yikes" under her breath during the stress level assessment) is not so easily dispersed. Great pockets of adrenaline, stored in anticipation of the weigh-in, release at intervals following its anticlimax. When night comes, I sit in bed, trying and failing to sleep. A snifter of fortified wine seems like the obvious solution, but the parameters I've set for myself regarding its consumption require it to remain corked until Friday evening.

Instead, I bring my kettle down the hallway to the bathroom to fill with the intention of making tea. Only, when I return, I am once again struck by how empty the room looks. Maybe it's all of the extra time I've been spending here due to the early termination of our workdays. Or maybe it's the hour: in the darkness of night, the lamp on my bedside table works so hard to illuminate so little. Maybe it's the shame I'd felt when the health specialist visited me so often this past weekend brought back to the surface by the excess energy running through me. Whatever the reason, the sparseness of this room, the one corner of the Institute I can call my own, disgusts me.

So, despite it being the middle of the night, I leave in search of some accoutrements to make my quarters feel a bit more like home. Though "search" really isn't the word. Our work here has been nothing if not a cataloging of furniture constructed for anonymity. Really, there is one place to go, the closet on the first floor where we deposited all personal items we found our first week here, and even this provides little in the way of décor. I search through its assortment of random items left behind, and I am almost ready to conclude there is nothing worthwhile when my flashlight reflects off the glass of a picture frame. Moving aside several buckets, I find the photograph of the researchers.

Several men and women wearing white lab coats stand in two rows on a raised platform against a wall, one that is mostly white but blotched here and there with gray shadows. In front of them is Kay. She sits at an angle, on a wooden chair that it takes me a moment to recognize as the one I reduced to pieces. Which is how I come to realize the background is not a white wall after all. It's the massive window in the amphitheater.

I look at the researcher in the very center of the top row, and I swear I can see something. It might be a defect of the photograph, or a dark fleck of something on the lens. It might be an optical illusion created by the starchy, rigid texture of his collar meeting the smooth, rolling texture of the out-of-focus background. Or it could be that he's standing in front of something far off in the snow.

Whatever it is, it's microscopic. I squint, bringing the photograph so close my nose nearly touches the glass.

"Who is she?" comes a whisper from behind me, and I snap upright, my nails digging into the wood of the frame.

My various daytime conversations with Gilroy are never without unsettling aspects, but now, late at night, with him suddenly appearing next to me, the entire enigma of him seems more menacing. All of my previous questions about him are overridden with terrifying variations. Not "Where does he sleep?" but "Does he sleep at all?" Not "What does he really do here?" but "What might he be capable of doing here, in service of his 'research'?"

I want to run, to sprint down the hall to the stairwell and up the entirety of the six floors to my quarters, locking the door behind me. But the hallway seems to grow colder with his presence, as if he's leaking frigidity, and I find my joints locked, keeping me in place.

"Who is she?" Gilroy repeats.

I look from Gilroy back to the photograph. "That's Kay," I answer, tentatively. This feels like a test, one that I'd prefer not to fail.

"I know who Kay is," Gilroy says. "And that's not Kay."

I study the picture once more. Either my hands are trembling or I'm shivering. "It's not?"

"The woman who arrived this past weekend," Gilroy says. "Who is *she*?"

"Oh," I say, "that's the health specialist." Then, realizing Gilroy's scarcity this week, I add, "She's here only one more day, if you need anything from her. She deals with all manner of health-related concerns."

"I couldn't put her through that," Gilroy says.

"Put her through what?" I say.

"You have to understand, the cold attacks all aspects of one's well-being," Gilroy says. "And so, given my continual and willing exposure to it, my own health is essentially a cave of horrors, one in which I would hate to entrap someone who is not thoroughly prepared. Like this woman, for example, since, as you say, she is a broad practitioner, not one specifically attuned to dealing with the cold and its terrifying fallout. Honestly, it would be better for everyone if she did not know I was here."

"You look healthy enough," I say.

"My skin is a mere sheet," Gilroy says, "laid over a pit of cobras. Just taking my vitals could turn a straight-A medical student away from the field."

"Huh," I say. "Well, it's getting late, and I—"

"Wait," Gilroy says, indicating the photograph with a flick of his chin, "what have you got there?"

"This?" I say. "It's just something I found to add a little life to my quarters. Celebrate the history of this place, you know?"

Gilroy steps next to me and takes hold of one side of the picture, forcing me to relinquish my left hand. He points, tapping the glass. "There I am."

It seems, for a moment, he has deluded himself. There are a few similar features, but the man in the photograph is not gaunt like him. His shape actually resembles mine somewhat. I can see this even as he stands in the second row, the greater outline of his form blocked by another. But that's not all. There's something else that doesn't translate, something I can't quite place.

"That's Donnelly there next to me," Gilroy says. "We were suitemates and great friends. The others hated us. We were the pranksters of the group, you might say."

I look from the photograph to Gilroy standing next to me. "You?" I say. "You were a prankster?"

Gilroy smiles, and in that moment, it becomes clear why I did not recognize him in the photo: the man in the photo looks happy, and Gilroy never does. At least he didn't until this moment. "We used to get up to all sorts of hijinks, Donnelly and me. We had a game we'd play. It was a chess match, but every piece was a queen. Do you know what an entirely queen-driven game of chess is like?"

"Seems like it would be easier than normal chess," I offer.

Gilroy shakes his head. "On the contrary, it was pure chaos. A diabolical blood sport playing out across sixty-four squares. There was no king, mind you. One would win only with the total eradication of the opponent's queens. In the beginning, this happened naturally. One of us would leave our last queen in the line of fire without realizing it. But we both grew too skilled for that over time. Eventually, we had to find more creative routes to victory. One of us might get the other intoxicated, for example. Or, one might spike the other's coffee or tea with a laxative, sending him out of the room to the lavatory, at which point any number of moves could be made, that being another rule of queens-only chess."

"Huh," I say again.

"Really, though, the game was only the epilogue," Gilroy says. "We derived the most joy from the collection of the other queens."

"You couldn't just play with the understanding that all of the pieces on the board were queens?" I ask. I've never seen Gilroy like this, and despite my having wanted nothing more than to escape him moments ago, it now seems imperative that I keep this conversation going. His uninhibited insights unrelated to the cold could be valuable.

Gilroy laughs, and it sounds strikingly natural. "We could've, but that would take all the thrill out of it. And we didn't have to either. Every one of us had our own chess set. There'd been a mistake in the materials sent to us in the weeks leading up to our departure to come here. On a page instructing us about what to bring, one item listed was 'something to pass the time,' and another was 'chess set.' This was an issue of dictation, we found out upon our arrival. The page's author intended 'chess set' to be a parenthetical example of something that might be used to pass the time. But since it was given its own line, and since the positions we had been selected to fill were coveted in the field of research, we followed the instructions with the same thoroughness that had earned us that employment in the first place. The result was that, in every room of every residential suite, one could find a chess set, ripe for pillaging by Donnelly and me."

Gilroy taps the glass again, indicating a woman in the front row.

"That's Melling. Hers was my favorite queen. It was a simple wooden piece, perhaps hand-carved, but ultimately austere. Its appeal I'm afraid I cannot explain. Likely, it was tied up in an osmotic sentimental value, as it had been gifted to Melling by her favorite aunt, a woman named Ethel who possessed just a single eye. Whether she lost the eye to an affliction or in an accident—or, possibly, was born lacking it—we never knew, because Melling herself refused to learn the details. She had, as a young child, been too afraid to ask, and then, as her bond with Ethel grew in adulthood, it felt almost disrespectful to broach the subject. To ask the question that Ethel had likely spent an outsized portion of her life answering would be a betrayal of their ever-expanding sense of kinship. So devoted to Ethel was Melling that she'd bring her photograph with her to whatever room she'd been assigned to. We all called her 'the Cyclops.' The aunt, I mean, not Melling herself. Melling naturally hated this, but we intended it as a term of endearment. And I am being honest when I tell you that nothing brightened my days here more than seeing Melling assigned to the same room as me, and then scanning her surroundings, looking for Ethel's framed face. To meet her monocular gaze felt like receiving a sly wink over the hushed fracas of discovery."

Here it is, I think. My opportunity to learn something of value about this place, something that might inform our work and maybe even reveal some truth about the thing in the snow. "What kind of discovery?" I ask. "Were you still studying the cold back then?"

Gilroy ignores me. "Donnelly did not challenge me for Melling's queen whenever we set out to discreetly collect our pieces. He favored novelty over simplicity. And despite being men and women of precision, or perhaps because of it, he had his pick of ludicrous chess queens. Like Dawson's, for example."

Gilroy indicates a man at the far end of the second row. The man's expression is so intensely blank that I need to lean in to be sure he is not a mannequin.

"Dawson had a chess set wherein all the pieces had been fashioned to look like famous monuments," Gilroy says. "They were the basics, and that's how Dawson preferred it. He thought the purchase of airfare could be equated to culture and claimed to have traveled the world, when really he'd toured only the locales covered in the coffee-table books he likely owned. He would talk to us at length about a certain place he'd visited, showing us photos of this famous landmark or that, but if you asked him about engaging with the locals or straying from the beaten path to find someplace to eat, he would look at you, perplexed, as if unsure why anyone would do such a thing. He and Donnelly took the same helicopter here at the outset. Do you remember the mountain range? The one that separates this region from civilization?"

"I slept on the helicopter ride here," I admit, and immediately feel stupid.

Gilroy thankfully does not take this admission as a sign of my unworthiness as a listener. "They're beautiful. The mountains. Or maybe 'striking' would be a better word for them. Nary a tree graces a one of them. Just pure, jagged stone, unapologetic in its brutality. In the nightmares I have frequently, where the cold has taken on a physical form that chases me through the halls of the house I grew up in, it looks not unlike the miniature of one of those stark mountains. But that's neither here nor there. The point is, Donnelly noted that, as he leaned up to the window, hoping to snap a photograph of them, Dawson sat staring straight ahead, his expression unmoved. Donnelly took this to mean that Dawson did not possess an interest in nature's splendor. Suffice it to say, it confused him greatly as we all got to know each other and Dawson began referring to himself as a chronicler of the world, natural and man-made. But in the end, it made perfect sense. Dawson's taste in scenery, which he thought made him someone worthy of high regard, relied entirely on the experiences of travelers before him. As the mountain range had not been called beautiful in any of his guidebooks, he could not see it as such."

Gilroy taps a woman standing to Donnelly's right. She's tall, taller than both Donnelly and Gilroy, and smiles in a way that strikes me as both cheerful and tragic.

"Bradshaw," Gilroy says. "She had another of Donnelly's favorite queens, a ceramic piece with the head of an Irish wolfhound. The rest of the pieces were also dogs. The king, a Great Dane. The bishops, knights, and rooks, an assortment of collies and shepherds. The pawns, all variety of little dogs such as Chihuahuas and dachshunds. This bothered Bradshaw, as few of the pieces seemed to match up with her understanding of the breeds' temperament and desire for dominance. I forget the context in which this came up, but it must have been one of the only times Bradshaw spoke aloud about dogs. Her feelings for them were so strong, she could barely say a word concerning them without breaking down in tears, the root of her sadness being both the general lack of dogs at the Institute and, more specifically, the lack of a particular dog, a beloved heeler named Jepson, who she'd been forced to leave with her sister. So she celebrated her love of canine-kind entirely through possessions and apparel: buttons, hair clips, a handmade clay mug made to look like the head of a mastiff, that sort of thing."

The conversation lulls a moment, and I worry it might come to an end without anything resembling an answer to all the questions I have about this place. It feels forced to return to the research, so I focus on what compelled this monologue out of Gilroy in the first place: the photograph.

"And which one is the hiker?" I ask.

Without warning, Gilroy lets go of the frame. The side I'm holding slips from my hand, and it drops to the ground, but, miraculously, doesn't shatter. I reach down and pick it up before turning to Gilroy, who glares back at me.

"Who told you about the hiker?" he says, his tone suddenly severe.

"I read about it," I say, "under the tables."

"The bottoms of the tables aren't for you," Gilroy snaps. "They're not for anyone who cares about the truth."

I scan the faces looking for someone bold and maybe a little bit deranged. "So, there was no hiker?"

I wait for Gilroy's answer but none comes, and when I look up, he's halfway down the hall.

"Where are you going?" I call after him.

"I have work to do," he calls back.

"But it has to be one or two in the morning," I say.

"I know," he says, without raising his voice, so that I can barely hear him. "I've wasted too much time here." With that, he disappears around the corner.

I look at the photo as if it may provide some explanation of this sudden turn. The researchers only stare back at me, their eyes open but their mouths shut.

23.

On Friday, all that's left is the haircut and the mental health exam. After going last the day before, the others insist I go first, and I do not argue, eager for the week to be over.

Inside the conference room, the health specialist sets me up on a chair in front of a table with a mirror on it.

"So," she says, observing the two of us in the reflection, "what are we thinking?"

"Just a trim would suffice," I say.

"And your beard?" she says. "Would you like that trimmed too? Or shaved?"

The beard throbs angrily at this suggestion. The lights seem to buzz along with it, violently enough that I'm surprised the health specialist doesn't seem to notice, given her hobby of cataloging the Institute's most unfortunate aspects.

"No," I say. "Leave the beard. I prefer to tend to it myself."

The health specialist puts an apron over my sweater and begins. She uses only scissors—clippers are a premium package offering, I imagine—so her progress is slow but steady until she stops abruptly and steps away. From her duffel bag, she retrieves a collapsible easel, which she sets up. She then takes a stack of papers from a valise and places them on the easel facing away from me.

"I'm going to show you a series of images," she says, retrieving her notebook from the table, "and all I need you to do is tell me what you see."

I check my reflection in the mirror. "I was hoping for a little more off the top."

"We'll finish the haircut when we're done with this," she says. "Nontransparency, organic data, remember?"

I mumble an acknowledgment and she turns the first image. At least, I expect the first image. The sheet is blank.

"There's nothing on that one," I say.

The health specialist does not look at it herself to confirm this. She keeps her eyes on me and indicates her notebook with a slight nod. "Is that what you want your response to be? 'Nothing'?"

"I was just letting you know," I say, "that that one's blank."

"Okay, 'nothing' it is," the health specialist says to herself, scribbling pointedly in her notebook. "And this one?" She moves the blank sheet and turns over another page, revealing another blank sheet.

"I'm sorry, I don't think I understand the exercise," I say.

"The way we respond to visual stimuli tells us a lot about our mental well-being," says the health specialist.

"But there are no visual stimuli," I say.

"Why do you feel that way?" she says.

I gesture to the page displayed, and in doing so knock hair loose from my smock onto the floor. "Because there's nothing there."

"So, we're going with 'nothing' again." The health specialist makes a notation in her notebook and removes the page from the easel.

"Wait," I say, "can I see that again?"

"No," says the health specialist.

"What about the first one?"

"No," says the health specialist. She takes the corner of the next sheet, but pauses. "Now, this is the final image I'm going to show you, but there's no time limit here. You can look at it for as long as you want."

Once again, I am greeted by a blank sheet. But I take the health specialist's words to heart. I take my time and look—and I mean really look—and after a few moments, I do start to see something. Or, more accurately, something reveals itself, not to my eyes but to my senses. Staring at the blank page on the easel, I see it transform from paper to white snow, and from white snow into a thick cloud, one of such dense, tight wisps, it is nearly solid, denser than even those that block the sun and moon here.

But what I am looking at is not a meteorological phenomenon. I slowly come to realize that it's a cloud of the mind, the cloud I find myself wandering blindly through each weekend, the cloud that obscures the order of things, the cloud that hangs over my memory and makes it difficult to recall any golf-ball-related anecdotes from my past, the cloud that erases entire evenings as I stand in my office with my eyes closed considering whether one of my subordinates has surpassed me, the cloud that renders visits from the health inspector—a break from routine that should've been eagerly anticipated—a surprise. To stare so directly into it, this thing that has been my enemy for as long as I've been here, scrambles my fight-or-flight instincts, so that I desire two things simultaneously: first, to stand from this chair, march to the easel, and tear it apart, thus freeing myself from its haze; and second, to shut my eyes tight, and crawl blindly until I locate the door and let myself out. The equilateral pull of these two possibilities means I remain locked in my chair until the health specialist makes a harsh snorting noise, drawing my attention to her. After examining the page so closely, the sudden detail of the room leaves me feeling light-headed.

"Sorry," she says. "Air's really dry here."

I want to ask her how long we've been in this room. The light quality from the window gives no hint of the passing of time.

"So?" says the health specialist.

"So what?" I say.

"So, what do you see?" says the health specialist.

I turn back to the easel to fully articulate my thoughts, but the page has reverted back to being merely a blank piece of paper.

"There's nothing," I say.

The health specialist makes a notation. "Three 'nothings,'" she says to herself.

153

I stand from my chair.

"Where are you going?" the health specialist says, putting down her notebook.

"What?" I say. "Are there more images?"

The health specialist picks up her scissors. "We haven't finished your haircut."

I look at myself in the mirror she's set up. My hair is trimmed on one side but long and straggly on the other.

"Yes, of course," I say, turning back to the health specialist. "I know. I was just stretching my legs."

24.

That evening, I meet the health specialist in the hallway outside her room to formally see her off. To simply allow her to leave seems unprofessional.

"When does it get here?" the health specialist says, meaning the helicopter. She's impatient to leave—already dressed for the outside, with her two large duffel bags neatly packed—and I will be happy to see her go.

"Eventually," I say.

"It doesn't come at an exact time?" the health specialist says.

"It has to do with weather conditions," I tell her, unsure if this is true.

The door to the suite opens and we both turn to find Gibbs peeking in. "I think I hear it," she says.

"Finally," the health specialist says, and she pushes past to follow Gibbs, leaving me to take her bags. In the hallway, I observe the two of them embrace.

"It was really wonderful to meet you," Gibbs says.

"And you," says the health specialist. "Keep in touch, seriously. I can't wait to see what you're able to achieve."

"You're too kind," Gibbs says, and the health specialist pushes through the door to the stairwell. She does not check to see if I'm following.

I give Gibbs a nod of acknowledgment and move to follow, but she stops me. "They'll drop off the folder for next week tonight, right?"

"Yes," I say. "Of course."

"But we won't see it until Monday," she says.

"Yes," I say.

"Not even you," she says.

"That's right," I say. "I like for us to experience the folder as a team."

"Great," Gibbs says. "Have a good weekend."

And as she leaves, heading to her own quarters, I arrive at a new theory for Gibbs's entire portfolio of behavior this week: blocking the thing in the snow, leading us away from it, befriending the health specialist. When the identity of the thing in the snow is finally revealed, she wants to savor it as an achievement of her descriptive competence. So she bonded with the health specialist, but also understood her—generally, as an outsider, and more specifically, as one who works in health, a field brimming with difficult-to-identify objects and devices—as a sort of threat. Were the health specialist to identify the thing in the snow before Kay's response could come, it would deprive Gibbs of the potential glory. I marvel at this the entire way up the stairs.

It isn't windy outside, but the helicopter's rotors swirl the air so that, when the health specialist holds the door open for me, we're hit with an intense gust of pure cold. I hand her bags to her and say, nearly shouting to be heard over the whir of propellers, "I'm not allowed out on the roof when the helicopter's here."

"What?" the health specialist asks.

"I'm sorry," I say. "The roof protocol is very clear, and this, unfortunately, does not constitute an emergency."

She grimaces at this and leaves, letting the door slam shut behind her. And I hate to admit it, but her departure feels like a small victory after a long week, one that I relish standing there at the top of the stairs, waiting for the helicopter to lift off. But it doesn't. A moment later the health specialist is back, without her bags, and with a new expression, one of exhaustion. The vestibule fills again with noise and cold.

"The paperwork," she says. She holds out two manila folders.

"What?" I say. "I usually pick that up on Monday."

"The pilot says you forgot to fill out the week's paperwork," she says. "Looks like it's only one line, though, so if you have a pen—"

"We had an assignment?" I say. "But it was wellness week."

"We ended before lunch each day," the health specialist reminds me.

Of course. This is all I can think: Of course Kay would expect us to work after the health checks. Of course she wouldn't leave us to fend with hours of undefined time. Of course.

I begin to ramble about putting together a plan to get back

on track, but she doesn't care. She's not of this place. She just holds out the two folders, a parting gift worthy of this terrible week, until finally I stop talking. I take them, and then, at last, she leaves for good, or at least for six months, however long that might be.

25.

Another weekend at the Northern Institute.

To return the folders to the lockbox only to take them out in two days seems like a waste of time. But I would like to keep my promise to Gibbs that I will not look in them until we reconvene on Monday, and I would also prefer not to spend the weekend contemplating the week ahead. So I set the folders on top of my bookshelf and leave them there.

What follows is a terrible limbo in which the question "What comes next?" seems both answerable and impenetrable. As I sit in bed, drinking tea, my eyes repeatedly drift and land on the folders. Several times I leave the warmth of my bed under the pretense of using the bathroom, only to stand there, next to the small bookcase, staring down at them, wanting and also not wanting their blank, off-white exterior to reveal something to me. But I do not open them. I do not even touch them.

. . .

I anticipate that the others will take issue with there suddenly being two tasks to complete in a week. To admit fault in this situation seems unwise, given how much authority I ceded during wellness week—necessarily to the health specialist and unnecessarily to Gibbs, in terms of room selection. Indeed, it wouldn't be unreasonable to say that the news of the added workload could leave me vulnerable to a full-blown coup. Therefore, I decide it best to frame the extra task as a positive: Kay has been so impressed by our progress she's decided to give us additional work, knowing we can handle it. The only thing I lack is a message from Kay expressing this much.

Just a few weeks ago I might have considered it immoral; now I decide my best course of action is to forge a Post-it expressing her high regard for our effort level.

It is not difficult to find her last message. Gibbs left it at the corner of the desk in my office, presumably to be used as a source of motivation. Digging through the drawers, I find one more correspondence that I for some reason did not throw away. It reads:

> H.,
> Re: dead outlet, leave be; potential hazard/insurance issue.
> —K.

I don't recall writing whatever note inspired this response, nor any outlet-related issues, but considering how much my grasp on time has loosened, I don't bother trying to dredge up the memory. I take these notes to my quarters, sit at my desk with my blanket wrapped around me, and begin my work. I stick the notes to the surface, and lay down a flimsy notebook page over the top of them, ready to trace.

The message must begin with a note on our performance before moving into the unfortunate news of additional work. I decide to keep it straightforward: *You're doing great work.* Immediately, though, I run into a problem: neither of Kay's messages gives me a *Y* to work with. I attempt first to simply write my own, but it appears ragged and strange next to the other letters, the clearly guilty party in a lineup of innocents. Next, I try to attach a lowercase *l* (nothing more than a straight line in Kay's unadorned hand) to the bottom of a *v*. The result is a *Y* of freakish height, towering over its fellow letters in a way that seems more grotesque than ludicrous. Subsequent attempts wherein I stop tracing the *l* partway down all look curtailed in a similarly disquieting way. Using the curved hook of her simple lowercase *g* creates a *Y* that is far too dainty and ornate, like a tuxedo among tracksuits.

I decide to take the note in a different, *Y*-less direction. I try to really channel Kay's voice and come up with the following with the letters at my disposal:

- *Re: great worK as of late; more now*
- *Re: second tasK; can handle due to great worK*
- *Re: recent performance: good; additional assignment added*
- *Re: good worK these days; can do more*

- *Re: high performance in job; result is more tasKs*
- *Re: second tasK; result of good job*

Having only a capital *K* to work with really throws things off, and also I cannot seem to write a message wherein this new arrangement doesn't seem like a punishment.

I continue toiling with this throughout the weekend.

When I need a distraction, I read.

In this book of the Leader series (*On Shaky Ground*), Jack French finds himself sequestered in a resort that takes up the entirety of a small island. Finally, he can put pen to paper and complete a draft of the book he hopes will teach the world his ways of effective management. Thinking he will have nearly two weeks on the island to begin the writing process, he spends the first three days wandering the beaches to center himself. It is during these strolls, which frequently take place before noon, that he observes two men and a woman occupying stools at a small open-air bar on the beach. They speak loudly and obnoxiously and appear entirely intoxicated despite the early hour.

It is on a late afternoon walk, though, that Jack French finally has his breakthrough: the perfect opening line to his book. This, apparently, has been something holding him back. At his previous stops, it is explained, he had only been taking notes and thinking through the book's overall structure. (This feels like revisionist history, but to consult previous installments seems dangerous, given the weekend's ability to rearrange time.)

The reader does not learn the line at this time, only that Jack French rushes to his room, records it on a piece of paper, and then proceeds to the same open-air bar he has passed many a morning to have a celebratory cocktail. Here, he learns from the bartender that the members of the boisterous group he sees there so often are actually three government officials from a small city back on the mainland. As the bartender understands it, they've made the trip using taxpayer money allocated for renovations to their local river walk. This causes Jack French considerable consternation, as there is nothing he hates more than poor leadership, but he decides to leave it be. After all, he has his own work to do.

Of course, he never manages to write a single word beyond the first line. Later that evening, he finds himself in the resort's laundry facilities, pressing some wrinkled shorts from the bottom of his suitcase, when who walks in but the three aforementioned officials. They are completely inebriated and unsure of where they are. Jack French sighs, ready to help them back to their rooms, but the moment he sets down his iron, a massive earthquake strikes.

The remainder of the book involves Jack French's quest across the island (and through a monsoon) to a tower where he can radio to the mainland for help, stopping frequently to help those who have been injured or otherwise inconvenienced by the disaster. He makes this short yet treacherous journey alone, as he finds the government officials impaired in both judgment and courage. Still, when he finally is able to contact emergency services, he inexplicably refuses to identify himself, saying only that he could not have done it without help from the three of them.

Once emergency services have arrived, he goes back to his room and finds that the window has broken and the rain has blown in, soaking the notepad on the table beside the bed, erasing it, just as the night's various stresses have erased it from his mind.

Only in the epilogue do we hear about the aftermath of the government officials. Jack French had counted on their narcissism driving them not only to confirm their nonexistent involvement, but to embrace it. In the ensuing media coverage, though, it becomes clear just how little they had done. Moreover, their appearance together at a tropical resort raises questions about how they had afforded such a thing, prompting an investigation that ultimately exposes their financial malfeasance. This makes it unique in the Leader series, in that Jack French does not lead them but rather exposes their own faulty leadership.

I try not to think about what Jack French would say about my attempts at forgery.

The photograph of the researchers is on my desk, propped up against the wall because I have nothing with which to hang it. Occasionally, working on my note, I look up at it, attempting to channel Kay. More often, though, my gaze drifts toward Gilroy, trying to connect the man in the photo with the man who wanders the halls of the Institute, before I move to the researcher in the middle of the top row.

What is it, that little mark? Is there something out there behind him, or is it just a defect in an old photograph? I stare at it, leaning across my desk to get a closer look, but it seems to resist identification. Every time I decide it's just a printing error, some new edge reveals itself. And every time I think I see some definitive shape, it's as if it blurs. The mystery of it warps my basic understanding of photography, and I catch myself leaning this way and that, trying, in vain, to see around the man.

This eventually frustrates me. I get up and pace the room with my blanket still wrapped around me, and once again I catch sight of the folders and stare at them.

It's on this occasion that three things occur to me in rapid succession: first, that one of the folders contains an additional Post-it from Kay, explaining the thing in the snow; second, that it's possible this note could contain a *Y*; and third, that I will not, under any circumstances, look at the note until Monday, and need to abandon my own note. The double betrayal—the forgery and lying to Gibbs about waiting to open the folder as a team—would be too much. Not to mention, it would seem suspicious for Kay—a maestro of efficiency—to have used two Post-it notes to convey a pair of messages that, in all likelihood, could easily have fit on one.

Freed from my task, I think to take a few laps or get some more rest, only for the clarity of Sunday evening to arrive so suddenly it gives me a minor headache. I've spent the bulk of my two days off working on the Post-it and I have nothing to show for it. And still, the sad truth is, aside from the lack of physical movement, this weekend has been no more a waste than any previous.

In this way, another weekend at the Northern Institute passes.

26.

The other two are already waiting in the hall when I arrive at my office on Monday morning. Their excitement is palpable; they have apparently spent the weekend anticipating the contents of the Post-it within and its explanation of the thing in the snow. What proceeds is a quiet, tense coffee hour, one during which Cline and Gibbs steal what they believe to be covert glances at the folders on the table.

There is little to talk about, but the room is not silent. The buzzing of the overhead light fixture, flipped on to combat the morning gloom, fills the space, growing slightly louder with each passing minute.

I eventually start speaking, just to cut through the noise. "Well, it's a good thing we had so much free time after each morning's wellness checks last week. Based on the number of folders in the lockbox—not that I've opened them—it appears—"

Cline's attention snaps from the folder to me. "Wait, we're doing more health stuff? Isn't that kind of overkill? Not that health isn't important—"

"No," I say, "there will be no more health checks. I was just saying, I hope you both took ample advantage of your free time, as it appears we might be busy—"

"It's nine." Gibbs points to the clock mounted above the door. "We should probably get to work."

"Yes, certainly," I say, "and we shouldn't waste a minute because, as I'm sure you've noticed, we appear to have a second—"

But Gibbs has already put down her mug, moved across the room, and flipped the top folder open, pulling the Post-it off the page within.

"What does it say?" Cline asks with a conspiratorial hush.

Gibbs does not respond. She stares at the note for a bit too long, her expression proceeding from confusion to frustration and then to flatness. Finally, she hands it to Cline, whose face conveys a similar series of emotions.

This, I had not expected—that the distraction of the thing in the snow might finally be coming to an end. I'd internalized the hysteria of the others, and could not see the Post-it bringing anything but more of the same—excitement, speculation, distraction. But judging by Gibbs's and Cline's disappointment, it's possible that what it has actually brought is an end to their fun.

"May I see?" I ask, trying not to sound too excited.

Cline hands me the Post-it. It reads:

H. & all,
Re: thing in snow—if immobile, not of concern.
—K.

168

I read it three times, but with each pass, I find myself more confused. The only thing that is certain is that the note would not have helped me with the forgery. "No Y." It takes me a moment to realize I've spoken out loud, and my body tenses.

But Gibbs only snatches the Post-it from me as if she owns it, saying, "Exactly. No why. No what. No anything."

"Well," I say, "it might not be the resolution we were looking for, but at least we know that the thing in the snow is not something we need to worry about."

"If it's immobile," Gibbs adds.

"Which it is." I leave a pause for affirmation of this simple and observable fact, but receive none. "At any rate, we should do our best not to dwell on it, especially not this week, as we've been given an additional—"

"Why are there two folders?" Cline asks.

"Because we have two tasks this week," I say. For the second time in just a few moments, I pause, allowing for follow-up questions.

"Huh," says Cline.

"Weird," says Gibbs.

And that's as far as the issue is discussed.

We decide to focus on one assignment at a time, leaving the second folder closed until we can finish the task outlined in the first: to check the blinds.

Specifically, our instructions are to ensure that each blind will "lower and remain lowered after two or fewer pull attempts," and will "retract high enough so as to leave the bottom two thirds of the window exposed, with three or fewer pulls." She asks us to test the blinds three times each so we can be sure of their structural verisimilitude, or lack thereof.

I insist that we begin on the first floor with the Cubicle, as this seems logical. Upon beginning our work, though, I realize the futility of this: pulling blinds on windows that look out upon nothing but hard-packed snow. Nevertheless, I do not insist that we move to the third floor, as the instructions make no mention of the first two floors being precluded from the task. And so, in a vacuum of pointlessness, distraction festers.

We're only two rooms in when Gibbs starts dwelling on the note from Kay.

"I'm having a hard time figuring this out," Gibbs says, standing in front of a window.

"Try not to pull so hard," I say. "Sometimes the lightest tug results in the greatest retraction." I am only given a moment to admire my own unintended poignancy.

"I mean, I'm having a hard time with figuring out what Kay meant," she says.

"It seems straightforward to me," I say. "The thing in the snow is immobile, so we shouldn't worry about it."

"But that's not what she said," Gibbs says. "She said, we shouldn't worry about it *if* it's immobile."

"Which it is," I say.

"Correct," Gibbs says. "As of right now, the thing in the snow is immobile."

"And it has *been* immobile," I say, "since we saw it."

"Well," Gibbs says, "it did just show up one day."

"I thought that it was uncovered," I say.

"That's one theory, yes," Gibbs says.

"Your theory," I say.

"I don't think the theory belongs to any one of us," Gibbs says.

"It was yours," I say. "You came up with it, remember? Because we first saw the thing in the snow after that windy night, when the wind—what was it? Blew hard enough to put out a candle through a closed window?"

Gibbs turns from the blind she's working on and narrows

171

her eyes at me. "Where are you from? I didn't realize that was a saying outside my hometown."

"It's not," I say. "You told us about it."

"I did?" Gibbs says.

"I've definitely heard it before," Cline says.

Gibbs blinks hard to dismiss the talk of wind and unseen size. "Look, my point is, it's weird, what she said. One of two things is happening here. First possibility: she doesn't know what it is, and she's just saying, as long as it doesn't move, it's not a problem, because, as a rule, things that don't move aren't as concerning as things that move."

"That's why people love still life paintings so much," Cline offers.

"What?" I say. As usual, Cline has mistaken a desire to interject for a need to.

"Still life paintings," he says. "You got some flowers. You got some fruits. But there's no movement to speak of, which means there's nothing intimidating. Unless you're allergic to one or more of the fruits or flowers. But even then, it's like, buddy, this is as close as you're going to get to this stuff without a trip to the hospital, you know? Which isn't to say there aren't any subversive still life painters out there, but even then, there's a comfort in the promise that all the things are gonna stay put."

"What's in a subversive still life?" I say.

"Honestly," Cline says, "some of the still lifes I've seen? I don't even want to say the stuff out loud."

We pause to consider this before Gibbs presses on.

"The *other* possibility—"

"Yes," I say.

"The other possibility," Cline says.

"Is that she does know what it is," Gibbs says. "And she knows it's capable of movement. Otherwise, she'd just say, 'Don't worry about that thing; it's not going anywhere.'"

"If Kay knew what the thing in the snow was, she would tell us," I say. "After all, she's entrusted us with the care of this place. She'd want us to know."

"She didn't tell us about the rash," Gibbs says. "She didn't tell us about the hiker, or that some people are immune to the snow sickness."

"What?" I say. "How do you know about that?"

"Cline told me," Gibbs says.

"When?" I demand.

The question perplexes Gibbs. "I don't know. Some weekend?"

"You see each other on the weekends?" I say.

"Yeah," Cline says. "What else are we supposed to do?" Then, a look of panic flashes across his face. "Wait, is that not allowed?"

"Of course it is," I stammer. "I just prefer to spend weekends alone, what with how time can be."

"What do you mean, 'how time can be'?" Gibbs says.

"How it gets muddled," I say. "On the weekends."

"Muddled?" Cline says.

"Oh come on," I say. "You know what I mean."

The others only stare at me.

"I used to ask you what you did on the weekends and you

wouldn't be able to answer." It comes out pleading, but the others don't give in.

"We don't do much," Cline says, just as Gibbs says, "We don't have to tell you what we do when we're not working."

"So you have no time-related issues on the weekend?" I ask, incredulous.

"Sometimes it goes by fast," Cline says. "Sometimes not so fast."

The topic isn't worth pursuing if the others aren't going to be honest about it. "At any rate, this is different than something written under the table about a rash or a hiker," I say. "We've asked directly. If she had more to tell us, she would've put it in her message."

"So you're saying she doesn't know what it is," Gibbs says.

I open my mouth to counter this and realize what a perfect trap Gibbs has set. Either the thing in the snow is something Kay can name but chooses not to, which makes it worthy of our fascination, or something she cannot name, which makes it perhaps even more worthy of our fascination. And despite the logic to this, I don't like the avenue this opens—one wherein we may slander our superiors—both for Kay's sake and for my own.

I measure my words and speak slowly, to be sure my subtext is not lost. "What I'm saying is, Kay perhaps could not discern the identity of the thing in the snow based on your description."

Gibbs stiffens at this, but does not back down. "Then why no follow-ups?"

"Maybe Kay, as our employer," I say, "understands the

potential pitfalls of getting too wrapped up in solving the mystery of an immobile object—"

"Currently immobile," Gibbs interjects. "As far as we can tell."

"—out in the snow, and doesn't want us to get too distracted from the work we're paid to do." I feel a smug sense of satisfaction when Gibbs can't seem to find a rejoinder to this, until I realize the morning is already over and we've barely made any progress at all.

28.

The conversation dies down, but the silence does not bring us back to the task at hand. The others are distracted, and I find myself distracted by their level of distraction, stealing glances to check their progress and slowing my own in the process. It is not that they simply stand there, refusing to work. Rather, the tedium works like hypnosis. They successfully pull down and retract each blind three, four, five times in a row. Only when I pointedly clear my throat do they snap to attention and begin an assessment in earnest. This frustrates me, and I have no possible outlet beyond the blinds, which I then yank too hard, sending them up when I'd like them to stay down, or grounding them when I'd like them to retract.

Similar to our other tasks here, the day's work offers a new, if somewhat unexciting, framing of our space. Inhabiting the Institute has often felt like living in an enormous cement block, but over the course of the morning I have come to see it as a glass house. There are so many windows, sometimes as many as four in each room.

"Have there always been this many windows?" I don't mean to say it aloud.

"Yeah," Cline says.

"I know that," I say. "It's not like there would be more windows than when we arrived."

"No," Cline says, "I was agreeing with you. Like, there are a lot of windows."

"Tons," Gibbs says absently, without turning from her blind.

We don't make it all the way through the first floor by five. I dismiss the others as soon as they begin eyeing the clock, adding that I will stay and keep working. My hope is that one or both of them will also remain behind so that we can make adequate progress for the day, but neither volunteers, and so I am left alone, at which point I realize that my own preoccupation with Gibbs's and Cline's inefficiency was the only thing keeping me going. Without them to monitor, I am easy prey for the blinds' spell. Pull down, and the blind covers the window. A quick tug, and the blind retracts. A menu with two items, each a different hue of blank, perfect for lulling even the most determined practitioner into a state not quite like sleep, but not like wakefulness either.

I wonder: Do the mechanisms of a retractable blind deteriorate without use? Which is really to say, I wonder: Will we be asked to complete this task again? This only opens the door for another thought: Have we done this *before*?

I try to call up some recollection of this, but it is a task that seems custom built to withstand the creation of a memory. It would not be repressed like something traumatic. Instead, it's as if the act of forgetting coincides with the action itself, almost like there's no difference between it happening and not happening. And yet, the sheer quantity of blinds to pull and retract seems like something that would easily register in the memory—monotonous as it is, could one truly forget a task so dull and time-consuming as methodically testing blinds? Though that raises the question, would the nature of this work—its volume, its monotony—propel it straight past a casual memory into the arena of trauma, where it would likely be repressed?

The questions only beget more questions, so I try a different approach. I attempt a full assessment of our time here at the Northern Institute. The trouble is, I can only seem to think of things from these past several weeks. I can remember with clarity the day of the thing in the snow's discovery and those that followed it, but the time preceding it remains foggy. Some minor things present themselves—naming the rooms, rounding up the personal effects and putting them in the closet on the first floor—but I cannot come up with anything more substantial. I remember Cline waxing philosophic over the concept of "shine" while wiping down windows. I remember discussing if a clog (of the plumbing variety, not the ear canal) constituted only a complete backup of all water and waste, or if it was a spectrum encompassing all levels of delayed flow. I remember distinctly Gibbs saying to me, "It's designed to go left to right; that's why it's leaving a trail," although I cannot remember the context. Going back further, to the interview with Kay or our onboarding sessions, I can recall almost nothing aside from the points essential in completing our duties. What sort of rooms did these things happen in? Were we shown a video? Were there icebreaker activities with the three of us back at headquarters or did we do those here? Even the memory I had dredged up last week—or, no, it would be the week before last—concerning the use of a golf ball to deal with arch pain, weak as it was at the time, now only exists in its spoken form, so that I can remember speaking of it, but I cannot remember experiencing it.

As I stand there, flipping between the blank of the white blind and the darker blank of the densely packed snow, a word flits through my mind: "Gone."

Then another: "Hey."

Then another: "Hello."

Then a hand obstructs my view, its fingers snapping to get my attention, and I startle to find Gilroy standing next to me.

"Is she?" Gilroy says.

"Is who what?" I say.

"The health woman," Gilroy says. "Is she gone?"

"Oh," I say. "Yes."

"Good," Gilroy says, "good."

I follow his eyes as they travel the length of my arm and come to rest on my fingers, which hold the blind, ready to tug. Releasing my grip, I say, "We're testing the blinds this week."

"Huh," Gilroy says.

"Have you been down here this whole time?"

"Just for the past week or so," Gilroy says. "Getting some work done."

"I thought you said the first two floors were like the basement," I say.

Gilroy smirks. "And I'm sure if you ran a broad survey of scientific breakthroughs, you would not find the basement as an entirely unrepresented venue. Besides, down here is best when it comes to studying darkness."

"I thought you studied the cold," I say.

Gilroy dismisses this with a simple gesture of the wrist. "It's all related. Sun, light, warmth, et cetera. But perhaps you're right. Without any health professionals around who would be intimidated by such a specimen as me, it might be time to re-surface. Not that there'll be much of a difference this late at night."

I'm about to let him know that it's only just after five and there might still be some daylight left, but a quick glance at the clock indicates that it's nearly nine. I look to the blind as if it might explain what happened to the hours, and by the time I return my attention to Gilroy he's nearly out the door.

"Wait, Gilroy, can I ask you something?" I call after him. He keeps walking. "Do you, or did any of the others, ever have memory issues here?"

In the doorway, he stops and turns back to me, a skeptical look on his face. "Why do you ask? Is that something you read under one of the tables?"

"No," I say. "I was just curious. You see, it's just that some-times, I can't remember—"

"Well, I can remember *everything* that's happened here," he snaps. He leaves without saying another word, but I understand clearly. There are things he wishes he could forget.

29.

We proceed through the first two floors slowly over the next few days. I am eager to move aboveground, but once we do, I realize the issue is the same: on three of the four sides of the building, the raising of the blinds reveals just as little as it did belowground, a slightly brighter array of nothing. It is on the fourth side of the building, though, that things begin to truly unravel.

"Hmm," Gibbs says in the first room on that dreaded side, looking out the window after a successful retraction.

"Interesting," Gibbs says in the second room.

"Very interesting," Gibbs says in the third room.

"That's not where I expected it to be," Gibbs says in the fourth room.

By the time we reach the Lookout, Gibbs is certain: "It's moving." Each time she speaks, it's in a stage whisper, an aside to herself that we are clearly intended to hear.

"No, it's not," I say.

Gibbs turns from the blind she's working on and looks at me with feigned confusion. "What's not what?"

"The thing in the snow," I say, "is not moving."

Gibbs turns from me to the window. "No, you're right. It's not moving."

"Thank you," I say.

"Right now, at least," she says. "But I think it moved when my blind was down."

"I was thinking the same thing," Cline says.

"Can we please just focus on the work?" I ask.

"Just do this one thing," Gibbs says. "Look at the thing in the snow. Keep your eyes on it. Then bring your blind down, retract it, and see if you're still looking at the thing in the snow when it comes back up."

Why I agree to this exercise, I'm not sure. It catches me off guard, I guess. I'm surprised Gibbs would even propose it, given how definitive it is. It seems obvious that it will disprove her own theory.

So we stand at separate windows, look at the thing in the snow, lower the blinds while keeping our eyes on the same spot, and then we give them a quick tug to initiate the retraction.

"Whoa," says Cline.

"See?" says Gibbs.

"Hold on," I say, "I wasn't focusing right. Let's try that again."

We repeat the steps. And we repeat them again. And a third time. It's as if the frames of the world's simplest animation have been randomly arranged. Each time, the thing in the snow is just to the left, just to the right, just above, just below where I've locked my eyes. My breath grows shallow.

"One more try," I say.

Gibbs sighs, but I go through with it anyway. This time I lean in as close to the window as I can get without the blinds hitting my face. My breath fogs on the glass, enveloping the only disruption on the landscape, and I frantically wipe it off with a sleeve. I then pull the blind down and loosen my gaze, hoping that, when I raise the blinds, my wider range of vision will reveal that it hasn't moved at all—that some part of this can feel natural. I take a deep breath and tug.

It works. The thing in the snow is in the exact same spot. It's as if I'm holding it in place. I stare at it, feeling victorious. And as I stare, I realize that, largely due to my losing the description contest, I have not actually observed the thing in the snow very closely in full light since my chair-obliterating leap to the stage some weeks ago. It is nothing more than a blight, I've told myself, something to acknowledge but not fully take in. Now its details present themselves with a disarming lucidity, as if a lens in my eye has been adjusted.

The slight buzz of the overhead light seems to grow louder, but I don't look up. I can't. The thing in the snow has me locked in place again.

The throb that runs through my beard at a low frequency increases in intensity, as if a dial is clicking up, up, up. I suddenly feel very sick. Is this what it does to the others? Or is it what it *did*? Am I simply experiencing the thrill of looking at it for the first time—standing still and truly looking at it, with no unfortunate landings to draw my attention away—an experience I will forever chase hereafter? Because that's what it is: an absolute thrill as the throb branches out, reaching every corner of my body. And yet, I know, deep down, that if I do not look away I will vomit.

As I cannot move my eyes, an expulsion seems inevitable, but luckily some synapse fires. I reach out, pull the blind down, and the sense of freedom is so intense I stumble back, coughing.

"Are you okay?" Cline asks.

"I just leaned very close to the window," I say, "which is very cold. The air hurt my lungs."

Cline does not sound convinced. "The air from the window? Hurt your lungs?"

"Did you see it?" Gibbs says. "It definitely moved."

"We cannot say it 'definitely moved' if we did not actually see it move," I say. "What's more likely is that our eyes moved while we were lowering and subsequently raising the blinds."

"So you saw it?" Gibbs says.

"Here's an idea," I say in lieu of granting her this. "How about Cline and I finish the blinds and you stay here and watch it?"

It's such a simple solution for everyone that I'm surprised when Gibbs nearly screams, "No!" The room is quiet aside from the hum of the lights as Gibbs takes a moment to compose herself. "I mean, I don't need to stop working. I just think we should let Kay know."

"We're not contacting Kay without more definitive evidence than we have," I say. And then, a thought occurs to me. "I'll be right back."

I make my way down to the closet on the first floor and retrieve a blue dry-erase marker. When I return, I retract the blinds and, careful not to look too closely at it, draw a circle around the thing in the snow.

"We'll check back tomorrow," I tell the two of them. "If it's not in the circle, we'll know, definitively, that it's moving."

The others seem satisfied with this. We make better time throughout the rest of the day, but it's not good enough. What is far more certain than the thing in the snow's mobility is that we are definitely behind.

30.

Friday's troubles start when the day is only an hour or two old. I awake from a dream in which the others keep insisting we check a sealed blue envelope Kay had sent along with the task for the week. It feels so real that I cannot get back to sleep, and eventually I decide the only way to put my mind at ease is to walk down to my office and check the folders to ensure the envelope's nonexistence.

On my way there, I pass the Lookout, where I am surprised to see a figure staring out the window, silhouetted by the dim glow of the window in contrast to the darkened room. Though the lights are off—or perhaps because the lights are off—I can tell that it's Gilroy. He is staring directly out at the thing in the snow, and for a moment I worry he might be locked in a stare just as I was. But no sooner does this possibility occur to me than he turns to leave. I duck into the next room, unseen, and wait for him to wander off before proceeding to my office.

There is, of course, no sealed blue envelope in the task folder.

This is a relief, but I cannot shake a lingering wave of anxiety. My mind is not fully awake. I can't fully access my sense of reason, so I struggle to snuff out the thoughts I would so easily spurn in the morning. Have I been summoned here? Yesterday, the thing in the snow seemed to paralyze me as I stared out the window. Might this "dream" be an attempt to lure me out of my bed, back into its grips? And, if so, what part does Gilroy play in the scheme?

It's ludicrous, all of it. With extreme concentration, I can see this. Still, on my way back to my quarters, I slip into the Lookout to check if the thing in the snow is even visible for Gilroy to have seen. The snow gleams in the sparse moonlight, highlighting the singular dark object at the center of a dry-erase halo.

Is it centered?

Careful to focus on the circle itself, rather than the thing in the snow, I see that it's sneaking under the sketched blue barrier. At least, it looks that way now. I'll admit, when I drew the circle originally, I did so hastily, an attempt to telegraph to Gibbs and Cline my lack of interest in this whole endeavor. But I thought I had given it some space. Then there is the matter of Gilroy standing here.

The allure of returning to sleep lends one confidence. The more decisive the conclusion, the quicker one can get back to the comfort and warmth of his bed. And so, as soon as this explanation occurs to me, I decide it is the only possible truth. Gilroy had said it himself: "We were the pranksters of the group, you might say," he'd said. "We used to get up to all sorts of hijinks, Donnelly and me."

Perhaps he lurked outside the Lookout while we were working, discerned the circle's purpose, and has moved it to rile us up. Whether he did so out of malice or affection does not matter. I cannot abide this. So I use the sleeve of my pajama top to carefully erase the circle, take the marker from where I left it on the windowsill, redraw the circle with the thing in the snow in its center, and return to my quarters.

In the morning, the others are already outside the door to my office when I arrive, whispering excitedly to one another. The energy makes me momentarily hopeful. Perhaps there is a way to leverage this enthusiasm for the purpose of finishing the blinds. Then, Gibbs speaks and my heart sinks.

"It moved," she says.

"What?" I say.

"The thing in the snow," she says. "It moved."

They lead me to the Lookout and, sure enough, the thing in the snow sits just outside of the circle. It takes some time to calm the two of them down. Naturally, they'd like to sit down and write a note to Kay immediately. Only after extended negotiations do they see what is clear to me: it would reflect poorly on us if we devoted time to such communication without finishing either of the week's two tasks.

"Let's try and power through the remaining blinds and decide how to address this at the end of the day," I say, dangling the prospect like a carrot in front of them. They agree, and I am once again given some hope.

But the day does not go productively. As was the case earlier in the week, each of us falls into a blind-testing hypnosis. Gibbs and Cline, I imagine, consider the possibilities of what this movement could mean. I, on the other hand, try to piece together the night previous. I thought I approached the window directly, examining the circle straight on, but could I have been standing at a strange angle? Might this have caused me, when I drew the new circle, to unwittingly encircle a swath of nothing? Throughout the day, during which we barely complete the third floor, I try to come up with an excuse to return to the Lookout and examine the circle. But I can think of none, so I consider further explanations.

Potentially, Gilroy returned to the room after me and redrew the circle once more, punishing me for my obstruction of his prank by making the movement appear even more exaggerated. And then, there is the final possibility he did not touch it at all, that what I am seeing is evidence of what Gibbs suspects: the thing in the snow is mobile. I try not to give this much thought.

The day's end arrives, bringing relief and dread. Gibbs wants to discuss what we'll tell Kay, but again, I point out the more pressing issue of our being behind—hardly close to finishing our first task, with a second task still hanging over us. When this does little to appease her, I offer to circle the thing in the snow anew and attach a line to the previous circle.

"How would that help?" she says.

"We can track the progress over the course of the next week," I say, "and thus have more to report."

Gibbs reluctantly agrees to this, and she and Cline bid me a good weekend and make their way to their respective quarters.

I return to my office, where I review the snow sickness symptom card for longer than usual. Could what we've experienced this week fit into any of these categories? Could my issues of memory be considered "disorientation" or "confusion"? The problem I finally run into is not that I cannot find a symptom to describe what's happening. It is with the statement at the top, which says definitively that the symptom should be something that occurs "for reasons I/they cannot explain." I know exactly why I'm struggling. It's the others and their harebrained obsession with the thing in the snow.

Ultimately, I put the card away, take a Post-it, and write the following note:

> Kay—
> Due to the misunderstanding concerning wellness week as well as
> a few distractions, we have not finished either of the tasks cur-
> rently assigned. This should not concern you, however, as we will
> meet all tasks, new and outstanding, head-on next week.
> Best,
> Hart

It fills me with embarrassment to write, an embarrassment that is only compounded when I realize, due to our lack of progress, I have no paperwork to attach it to, and must stick it crudely to the naked interior of the manila folder. After depositing this in the lockbox, I sit at the top of the stairs in my outdoor clothes and wait for the helicopter to come and go.

My expectation is this: there will likely be a note of repri-mand for our failure to complete last week's work, adhered to the coming week's task. So, while I do not like to retrieve the folders early, I think it will be best to receive Kay's disapproval as soon as possible. That way, I can take some time before the workweek to absorb the figurative blow and maybe even process it into motivation.

But when the whirling of the helicopter's rotors increases and retreats into the night and I step once again onto the roof, I open the lockbox and, oddly enough, find two more assign-ments, which I don't read, and no note from Kay. I guess I should be thankful not to be chastised, but what I really feel is forgotten.

31.

Another weekend at the Northern Institute.

Gilroy occupies my mind for much of the time. I'm certain he's the one behind the circle's slight (and then eventual not-so-slight) movement, proof be damned. Sitting in bed, wrapped in my blanket, I try to piece together a motive. Could it be some sort of experiment he's working on? The more we track the thing in the snow's movement, the more time we spend near the window, which is the coldest part of any room. Or maybe it could be an attempt to disorient us as the cold disorients him. Another possibility is that he might be studying how prolonged periods of staring at the reflective surface of the snow impact one's eyesight.

Of course, there's a more obvious answer here: the building is enormous, and yet it's clear that Gilroy would prefer to occupy it all by himself. This much is evident in how he treats each interaction with us as if he'll never recover the precious time we've wasted. And so perhaps this is all an attempt to frustrate the three of us to the point of voluntary self-termination.

The chances of catching Gilroy in the act of erasing and redrawing our circle are negligible. So I focus on gathering more general evidence. Which is to say, I take another tour of the tables.

I know Gilroy will not be named in any of the under-table entries, but I sense that he may be identifiable through actions alone: mentions of broad insubordination, manipulation, mischief, harassment of an emotional nature, something a step further from his admitted compulsion to steal queens as part of a modified chess game. The accounts I read are peculiar, but nothing of the sort that I'm looking for: the discussion of a researcher's laughter, which sounded indistinct from choking, causing the note's author to issue a warning to "employ humor with caution and diplomacy" in the subject's vicinity; someone referring to a board as a "wood-flat" on more than one occasion; more about the rash; more about the hiker; many messages shot through with insider lingo, rendering them incomprehensible to me, an outsider.

This lack of evidence regarding Gilroy's misbehavior frustrates me at first. But over the course of the weekend, it starts to seem like evidence unto itself. That none of the other researchers spoke of Gilroy's diabolical nature doesn't mean he does not possess one; all it might prove is his aptitude for concealing it.

There's plenty to read under the tables, but I still find time to go back to my room and start the next book in the Leader series (*The Color of Fear*).

I notice something peculiar almost immediately. Rodney Stuyvesant Jr. dedicated his previous books primarily to historical figures, as well as colleagues from the business community (and sometimes even other authors), praising them concisely for their guidance, personal or otherwise. This one, on the other hand, begins with something more sentimental.

FOR MY SON, Rodney Stuyvesant III, who made me a father and, in turn, taught me to be a better man.

I wonder briefly how old his son might have been at the time of this dedication, but the book itself seems to answer this question.

In it, Jack French reserves a room on a sleeper car of a train that will travel through a desolate tundra. There will be entire days between stops and very little scenery, which suits him, as the limited distractions will be perfect to finally get a start on his masterwork, the definitive treatise on effective management. This plan is interrupted, though, when the eccentric billionaire CEO of a technology company and his private army overtake operations of the train. As it turns out, he would like to use all on board as test subjects for an experimental new product: an ocular implant that allows one to finally see colors, in the CEO's words, "as they are truly meant to be seen."

Jack French quickly eludes the henchmen and retreats to the caboose, where he finds an encampment of other escapees. But they cannot simply flee the train, so treacherous and far-reaching is the surrounding wilderness. Thus, Jack French must assemble a small team of passengers to sneak through the cars and regain rightful control. The only ones to volunteer to come with him, though, are a young couple who are traveling with their infant son. When Jack French suggests they leave the child with the others, the two refuse, citing the importance of family.

The CEO's army, they quickly discover, has locked the doors to all of the subsequent train cars with computerized devices, each one possessing a more advanced code to crack than the previous. Luckily for Jack French, the young couple is no ordinary couple. They met at a university, where they both studied computer science, receiving high marks, until the unplanned pregnancy forced them to drop out and start a television repair business to make ends meet.

As expected, the two don't have much belief in their coding skills after so much time away, and also as expected, Jack French manages to give them one of his legendary pep talks, understanding implicitly what kind of leadership they require to excel. And yet, this happens very quickly. Other scenes of intrigue feel similarly rushed. A page or two here might be devoted to the group ducking under a table to avoid two soldiers on patrol, another page or two there to fighting a group of passengers who've received the implant, their newly expanded sense of color driving them into excited rages.

Much of the story instead revolves around Jack French's role in the group, which becomes to take care of the infant child. As it happens, every time the couple begins work to decode another lock, the baby starts crying. Entire chapters are given over to vivid descriptions of feeding the child a bottle, or changing his diaper, or making airplane noises to convert his cries into giggles as the father and mother work diligently off the page.

At the book's conclusion, order has been restored and all implants have been safely removed by a skilled surgeon who happens to be aboard the train. The couple tries to thank Jack French for his excellent leadership, but he shakes his head and lets them know that what he does is nothing compared to the pressure, and subsequent joy, that must define parenthood.

When I finish, I flip back to the beginning and check the publication date. The Leader series has been going for some time, and despite reading many of them, I still have only barely made a dent in the overall catalog. This book is nearly twenty-five years old, meaning if Rodney Stuyvesant III is the infant in the book, he's an adult now, likely as old as Gibbs or Cline.

And there's something about this that feels correct: as though, at the Northern Institute, in the time it takes to read a book, it might be possible for someone to age two and a half decades.

···

Aside from reading and searching for clues concerning Gilroy's potential for sabotage I embark on a new project: a chronicle of my weekend. Because if Gibbs and Cline can pretend to experience a chronological weekend, so too can I.

The idea is simple. The events of each weekend seem to reshuffle themselves as they happen, leaving me disoriented and unsure of any order beyond depositing the paperwork in the lockbox on Friday night at the outset and lying down to sleep on Sunday night at the conclusion. But what is stopping me from establishing a clearer chronology through brute force? By which I mean, I will keep a journal.

For purposes of clarity, the journal will be a series of simple notations of the weekend's happenings as they happen, devoid of any reflection. If I read, I will write:

I read my book.

If I go walking, I will write:

I go walking.

If I lie down for a nap, I will write:

I nap.

The idea is that an ordered list will stimulate my memory and at the end of the weekend I will be able to remember the previous two days in a more comprehensive manner than before, which might have a positive impact on my focus throughout the greater week.

The idea comes to me in the murk of the mid-weekend, at a time that is either dusk or dawn. Feeling inspired, I write, on a blank page in one of the notebooks I keep in my quarters:

I conceive of this journal.

And when I return to that notebook on Sunday night, this is the only entry I find. It is, oddly, in the middle of the page, giving more emphasis to how ridiculous the undertaking all at once seems to be. Time will always evade me on the weekends, regardless of whether I want it to or not.

I consider tearing the page out and throwing it away, but decide to leave it, as a warning to my future self, if I think to try this again. Which makes me wonder, were I to flip through this notebook, or any of my others, would I find other journal attempts, aborted after one nondescript entry?

I decide I don't want to know.

In this way, another weekend at the Northern Institute passes.

32.

Having ignored the folders aside from a quick check for a Post-it, I am surprised, Monday morning, to find two boxes in the supply hutch. One is small and unlabeled. The other is large and heavy and emblazoned with a company's emblem that looks somewhat like a tree, only futuristic.

I bring the small box down, start the coffee, and then return to the roof to get the larger one. When I get back, my face still feels cold as sweat gathers under my outdoor jacket. I have no time to change before Gibbs and Cline arrive.

"What is all this stuff?" Cline asks.

"We'll soon find out, I'm sure," I say, but Gibbs has already opened the smaller box and looked inside.

"A hair dryer," she reports.

"Maybe it's for a task," I offer.

"What would we need a hair dryer for?" Cline asks.

"I don't know," I say, and as this seems like a good enough excuse to turn the topic to work before the nine o'clock hour arrives, I add: "Let's take a look."

When I open the folder, though, the first sheet fills me with dread.

"What is it?" Gibbs asks.

"We need to assemble a chair," I say, "to replace the one that collapsed."

"How do you use a hair dryer for that?" Cline says. "Is there plastic to heat and bend or something? Because I don't think that should be my job if there is. I have a tendency to get a bit interpretive when it comes to shaping stuff."

"I imagine the hair dryer is for the other task Kay sent," I say.

"Two tasks?" Gibbs says.

"Yes," I say. "Just like last week. And we didn't finish either of those. So that means we actually have four tasks." Once again, I anticipate some questioning about this, and once again, there is none. The others accept the additional tasks without a thought, just as Kay seems to have accepted our lack of progress without any need to communicate her disappointment.

"Five tasks," Gibbs says.

"What's the fifth?" I ask.

Gibbs gestures to the window with her chin. "Tracking the thing in the snow."

"That's not a task," I say.

"It's important, though," Gibbs says.

"That it may be," I say, "but it's best, I think, that we not confuse our pet projects with official tasks."

"But wait, what are the tasks?" Cline asks. "There's the chair. And then we have to finish the tables from last week—"

"The blinds," I say.

"Oh yeah," says Cline.

"Tables were the week before last," I say.

"Of course," says Cline.

"Week before last was wellness week," says Gibbs.

"Ah," I say, "sorry, I meant the workweek previous to last week."

"Sure," says Gibbs.

"That was when we did the tables," I say.

"Yes," says Gibbs.

"And you wrote the description of the thing in the snow," I say.

Gibbs looks down into her coffee as if searching for some clarification. "Exactly. That's when I did that."

"Sorry," Cline says. "So it's the blinds and the chair and what else now?"

"Why don't we start with those," I say.

"So we finish the blinds?" Gibbs says.

"Yes," I say, but the mood is wrong. It'll be a repeat of last week, I can tell, with each of us getting lost in our thoughts and making very little headway. What we need now is something to accomplish, something that is a series of steps rather than a series of checks. "Or, we *will* finish the blinds," I say. "Eventually. First, let's take the morning and work on this chair. It might be nice to get something done and out of the way first thing. After all, how hard can it be to put together a chair?"

33.

It turns out to be very difficult to assemble a chair.

"How do you pronounce a *t* with an accent like that?" Cline says.

We didn't want to work in the amphitheater, given its additional coldness, so, having seen the pride she took in doing so during wellness week, I asked Gibbs to choose a room. She chose the Lookout, likely to monitor the thing in the snow's movement. Now the three of us sit on the floor around the parts from the box, each of us taking turns to study the instructions. We pushed the furniture to the walls to give us room to operate, and it is beginning to feel like a smug audience is looking on, each fully assembled piece mocking our lack of progress with its presence alone.

Gibbs takes the sheet from Cline, studies it a moment, and hands it back. "I think that's a four, but there are some print quality issues."

"Oh," Cline says, leaning in and squinting at the character. "Yeah."

This mistake can be easily forgiven, since the instructions

are written entirely in an umlaut-rich language we cannot identify, let alone understand. We must then use the diagrams as our north star, but while they show pieces labeled "A1" through "O7," we cannot easily discern which are which.

"B5 looks longer than F7," Gibbs says, holding two bars, "so I think this one is B5 and that one is F7."

I look at the diagram and at the two bars in her hands. "But neither of those have the hole at the midpoint."

Gibbs studies the two bars and then sets them down, frustrated.

"Okay, I've got these two together," Cline says, holding up his work to show us.

"That's a start," I say.

"The little piece is the tool," Gibbs says.

"What?" Cline says.

"I'm pretty sure that little piece is the tool meant for tightening the bigger pieces together," Gibbs explains.

"Dammit," Cline says, "you're right."

By lunch, we've managed only to identify which part will eventually be the seat part and which will be the back support. The rest of the chair remains a mystery, but as simply walking away would feel like admitting defeat, we keep at it, despite not even knowing which pieces comprise the legs.

"It's too bad we didn't keep what was left of the chair that collapsed," Cline says.

"That was an old wooden chair," Gibbs says. "I don't know how much it would've helped."

"I'm surprised they didn't send us another wooden one, then," Cline says.

"The paperwork asked only for a number of chairs that required replacement," I say. "There was nowhere to identify which chair it had been."

Cline and Gibbs nod at this. They are each of them trying to sort pieces by length and thickness. I watch them for a moment, making a mental note of their decision to speak of the chair's collapse passively, a gesture of kindness on their part not to draw attention to my involvement in the event.

It is late in the afternoon when Cline finally stands up, massaging his temples.

"I just can't," he says. "It's making me sick."

I look at him. "Nauseous?"

"Exactly," Cline says.

"Do you feel it in your stubble? A throb?" I ask.

"What?" Cline says, taking his hands from his head. "No, not really."

"Oh," I say, "of course."

"I'm talking about the diagram," he says, "of the chair. The one in the instructions."

"Yes, I know," I lie.

"It's worse than those ink things," Gibbs says.

"What ink things?" I ask.

"From the mental health exam," Gibbs says, "with the health specialist."

"Don't get me started on those," Cline says. "I had to have a whole talk with her about how not every shape needs to correspond to a thing, and how all I saw in each one was an artist at work in their desired medium, and how really it's not for me to say what it *is* as much as what it *means* to me, the likes of which I couldn't accurately express, not knowing the artist's motivation, so as to enter a conversation with them, figuratively speaking. She wasn't very happy with that, and I swear she took it out on me when she irrigated my ear."

"You had your ear irrigated?" I say.

Cline looks at the window, embarrassed. "It was platinum-level clogged," he mumbles. "We tried drops after the ear exam, but they didn't do anything, so she had to irrigate. It worked, but I swear I was off balance for the rest of the day after that."

"All my ink blots looked like boats," Gibbs says. "The first one I was like, 'That's a boat,' and then the next one I was like, 'That's also a boat,' and then the third one looked so much like the first two that I thought, 'I have to say this one looks like a boat too, or else I'm going to look like a crazy person,' which is the exact opposite point of the exercise."

The room goes quiet and I can tell the others are waiting for me to tell them about my experience with the mental health exam but understand that asking anyone, let alone a superior, to share such things would be taboo.

"Mine were blank," I say.

"Whoa," Cline says. "You had a blank one? That's interesting."

"No," I say. "All of them were blank."

"Huh," Gibbs says.

"So what did you say you saw?" Cline asks.

"Nothing," I say.

"Huh," Gibbs says again.

"There was nothing to see," I explain. I hope for some re-assurance, but neither one of them says anything else. Gibbs occupies herself with two rods, while Cline gets up and makes his way purposefully across the room to the tipped-over box the unassembled chair had come in, the larger of the two we'd received, with the indiscernible company logo on it. He picks something up off the floor near it, a small circle of paper.

"G6," he reads.

The box is tall and narrow. The instructions were in a plastic bag taped to the apparent back support. Now Gibbs puts down the rods, steps to the box, and lifts it with the opening to the floor. She gives it one shake, causing a small alphanumeric flurry.

"It's the labels to all of the pieces," she says. "Maybe they came unstuck in the cold?" Her voice sounds deflated, and I don't blame her.

It is not quite five, but we decide that this is as fine a place as any to stop for the day.

34.

Each morning, we return to the Lookout, and each morning, the others make note of the thing in the snow's meandering trajectory, drawing a circle around it wherever it ends up and connecting that circle to the previous with a line. This apparent evidence of mobility initially causes exhilaration, but as the week drags on, Gibbs and Cline grow disappointed by its aimlessness and its seeming refusal to come significantly closer. I perceive their attitudes changing, the thing in the snow transitioning from an object of excitement to a daily frustration, one preceding the grander frustration of our lack of progress in chair assembly.

Eventually, after two days of trying desperately to match the un-adhered stickers to their parts, we abandon the instructions, and go about using the "two-pieces strategy," a simple method devised by Gibbs wherein we each take two pieces at a time and try desperately to stick them together.

During these hours of fruitless struggle, one of us might suggest we turn our attention to the simpler and more straightforward task of testing the blinds. Progress here proves difficult as well; in the time we've taken to focus on the chair's construction, we have forgotten which room we left off on. The only blinds we can be sure we tested on the third floor are those in the Lookout, and even then, no one can recall if we finished after circling the thing in the snow. And so, as we mindlessly test the blinds in a room where the blinds likely have already been tested, the allure of the chair will draw us back to the Lookout with its potential for a breakthrough.

This return is sometimes rewarded. Or it will seem to be. We will all of us be sitting on the floor, our legs going tingly and numb on the cold vinyl tile, and a reassuring click will sound out from the set of pieces with which one of us is working, drawing the attention of the two others as if a siren had gone off. On these occasions, this newly combined piece will be put aside, and the work will continue with an air of resolute focus bordering on giddiness. The next morning, without fail, one of us will go to the successfully combined pieces, hoping maybe to siphon some of its success, to let it buoy us in our pursuit of other combinations like it—and we will find that they don't fit together as well as we thought. They will look bent. Or they'll wobble. Or one piece will fall off the other, clattering to the ground.

Cline and I receive these failures with disappointment and resignation, tossing the two pieces back into the greater pile without a word, but Gibbs does not accept things so easily. She'll spend an entire hour trying to reconnect what might never have been connected in the first place, her expression crestfallen and frenzied all at once.

The first time this happens, it saddens me to see. The second time, I grow frustrated with her inability to come to terms with the situation, but say nothing. The third time, on Thursday, she says, "I swear, they were totally locked together yesterday," and I feel stupid.

Gilroy! How has it not occurred to me that this could be his handiwork?

I'd already assumed his responsibility for the thing in the snow's "movement." The only reason I have not voiced the theory to the others is because I do not want to mention my own attempt to keep the thing in the snow contained, and also because the others, having grown so disillusioned by its lack of direction, rarely bring it up in conversation at this point. Gilroy's antics in this case are aggravating but not directly detrimental to our work. His decision to sabotage our progress with the chair is something else entirely.

That is why, at the end of the day Thursday, I brew myself a cup of coffee, gather the blanket off my bed, and quietly make my way to the Lookout. There, I huddle in the corner, sipping the coffee slowly to maximize the caffeine's release. I don't turn the lights on. I need to catch Gilroy in the act.

I can't deny that I'm excited. After such a frustrating week, the prospect of a confrontation, especially with someone as haughty and demeaning as Gilroy, exhilarates me. After some time, though, I grow impatient. Why is it taking him so long to appear? Then, finally, I begin to feel sleepy. The coffee has done its job. It has carried me deep into the night. Now a moment of decision has arrived: I can either get up, while I still have the energy and awareness to do so, or risk falling asleep right here, bundled up in my blanket on the Lookout floor, to be discovered by the others in the morning.

I decide on the former. After all, Gilroy does not seem to operate on the standard workweek schedule. There is nothing stopping me from resuming my stakeout over the weekend.

In my quarters, sleep arrives quickly, and just as quickly a noise snaps me awake. Half-asleep, I cannot identify what it was; despite its gargantuan size, the Northern Institute is a building like any other, capable of the kind of unnameable nocturnal groans and hisses that lead children to believe in ghosts. I lie there in the darkness, staring at what I can see of the ceiling. After a moment, my eyes droop and sleep approaches once more. Which is when I hear it again, clearer this time: a single stifled cough. Someone is in my room.

35.

I flip on the lamp on my bedside table and sit up, but do not leave the warmth of the blanket.

Gilroy sits at the desk, pen in hand, staring at a blank paper. "You wanted to see me?" he says.

"What are you doing here?" Why I keep my voice a sharp whisper, I can't exactly say. Maybe I don't want the others to hear me shouting. Or maybe I'm afraid of what Gilroy might do if I voice my true level of panic.

"You've been looking for me, haven't you?" he says. "Well, here I am. We have something to discuss, do we not?"

I don't know whether to express anger or terror, so I say nothing at all, sitting upright and holding the blanket with a tightness that, again, could be correctly attributed to either of the two aforementioned emotions.

"Fine, I'll get us started," Gilroy says in response to my silence. His countenance conveys both disgust and sadness. "It's me."

A slight thrill cuts through the cocktail of fear and frustration. I was right. It's been Gilroy all along.

But then he confuses things with a clarification: "It *belongs* to me."

"Wait, what belongs to you?" I say, and as I do, it suddenly dawns on me: I was right about the culprit, but wrong about the scope. It's been Gilroy all along, and not just with the window, not just with the chair. He planted the thing in the snow. He's responsible for all of this. "I understand."

"No, you don't," he snaps.

"How'd you do it?" I say.

"Do what?" Gilroy says. He seems suddenly impatient with me, as if he did not come here to confess the ruination of my team.

"Get it out there," I say.

"Out there? On my back?" He phrases this as a question, as if I should understand, and suddenly I do. All weekend, I'd been searching for the evidence of Gilroy under the tables, and he'd been right in front of me: he's the hiker.

"So it's not actually that large," I say, my grip loosening on the blanket. I am on the precipice, I realize, of finally knowing.

Gilroy lets out an angry snort. "You'd be the first to say that."

"Gibbs," I say. "She thought it was much larger and we were seeing only the tip."

"You talk about it with the others?" Gilroy says. He turns from the paper now and glares at me.

"I barely talk about it at all," I say. "But the others have been obsessed with it. Up until this week, it's been about the only thing they want to talk about."

"How have they even seen it?" Gilroy says, pleading.

"Through the window," I say.

Gilroy looks at his shoulder. "What window?"

"Just about any window on that side of the building," I say.

"What are you talking about?" Gilroy demands.

He's deflecting, I can tell. He's regretting this confession and wants to drive the conversation into the territory of absurdity. I must ask now, or I will lose my chance. I try to keep my voice as calm and steady as possible as I say, "What is it, Gilroy? Just tell me. I need to know."

Gilroy closes his eyes and lets out an exasperated breath. "A birthmark."

The answer hangs in the air a moment before I speak. "Did you say, 'a birthmark'?"

"Yes," Gilroy says.

"Are you speaking metaphorically?" I ask.

"What?" Gilroy says, opening his eyes. "No."

"I'm not sure we're talking about the same thing," I say.

"Of course you think that," Gilroy says, "because even after I told you not to believe everything you read under the tables, you couldn't help yourself. So you see all this talk of a rash, and you think, 'It's got to be a rash.' But I am here to tell you, having lived with it my entire life, that it is not a rash. It possesses no texture. It is not contagious. It is only a birthmark. That I can promise you."

Everything clicks into focus then. No, Gilroy is not the hiker, but he had been hiding in plain sight. Gilroy is the rash.

"I was talking about the thing in the snow," I explain.

"You saw something in the snow? Like, a person?" When Gilroy looks at me, his gaze is so piercing I must turn away.

"No," I say. "It's just a thing. Remember? I asked you about it before."

"Hm," Gilroy says.

"You've seen it, though," I say.

Gilroy shakes his head.

"I've seen you at the window, staring straight at it," I say.

Gilroy turns to my window now. "I have a tendency to get lost in thought while checking for precipitation."

"Oh," I say.

For once, I would welcome one of his abrupt, signature exits. Gilroy remains seated, though. His gaze moves from the window back to the desk, settling now on the photograph of the researchers propped up against the wall.

"I'd worked my whole life to get to a place like this, a place of scholarship and discovery, thinking it would be my escape," Gilroy says. "Every crude insult heaved by a bully on the schoolyard as a child, the stares of my peers during swim lessons, all the pain and loneliness, I thought it all a down payment on the eventual joy I would experience once safely with 'my people.' But what I learned here more than anything was that intelligence does not exorcise cruelty. It sharpens it. Or maybe that's not the right way to put it. It hides it, paints the insult with the veneer of truth-seeking. They playacted as if they were conducting experiments to get to the bottom of some great mystery. They'd touch my shoulder and attribute the texture of my sweater to it. They'd see me in the bathroom after a shower and posit that it was 'oozing.' Any fleck of dry skin on my sleeve would be proof of it scabbing over and falling off."

"And you couldn't simply tell them they were wrong?" I say, and immediately regret it. As if the solution to something this upsetting could be so simple and direct.

If Gilroy is insulted by the question, he makes no indication. "It went against the unwritten rules of the place. When we found ourselves alone in one of the rooms, awaiting some result or other, we'd slip under one of the tables and write a note. We understood that they'd be read, that there would be theories about who wrote what, but the notes could not be discussed openly. For some time, I thought the rash was someone else. Only when Donnelly came to me and demanded to see it did I realize they were all writing about me."

"Even your friend Donnelly," I say. I can't help but shake my head. "Gilroy, I'm so sorry."

"No," Gilroy says. "You've got it wrong. That's how we became close. He was the only one who really examined it. He called it beautiful. It was the first time anyone had ever ventured a compliment beyond calling it 'interesting,' a limp catch-all word that seeks to mean everything and in the end means nothing."

Gilroy seems to be waiting for some reaction to this, a rare social grace that I would like to reward (albeit one occurring after he entered my room as I was sleeping), but all I can think to say now is the newly forbidden word: "interesting."

I manage to mumble, "Oh," and Gilroy issues the slightest nod of the head to acknowledge this.

The room is quiet a moment, aside from the buzz of the lamp, pulsing in time with my beard.

"So you haven't been moving the circles?" I ask.

"The circles?" Gilroy says.

"The ones on the window," I say.

"That does not clarify things for me," Gilroy says.

"What about the chair?" I say. "Have you been fooling with it?"

"Again, I do not know what you're talking about," Gilroy says. "This, sitting here, is the first time I've used a chair in months."

"So it's not you," I say. "You're not trying to slow us down in any way."

"If I can be completely honest," Gilroy says, "I have no idea what is that you and the others do here."

"Okay," I say. And another pause. "Well, it is rather late."

"Do you mind if I stay here and get a bit of work done?" Gilroy says.

"I really should be getting to sleep," I say.

"I don't need the lights on," Gilroy says, and as always, there is no use in negotiating. I turn off the lamp and turn to the wall. For a short while, the frantic sound of his scribbling keeps me awake, but eventually, I fall into a fitful rest.

In the morning, Gilroy is gone, but he's left the paper behind. The words do not conform to the lines of the torn-out notebook page, but this is the only evidence that he'd written them in the dark, his handwriting otherwise neat, if a bit slanted with desperation. I pause to read some of it before I leave.

While the snow is not the cold's most merciless foot soldier, it is, in many ways, its most valuable. It is appealing to see, covering the gray death of grass in winter with simple, shimmering white. It gets in the way, inviting us to leave the safe warmth of the indoors to remove it. It lures children out of their houses to play in it, opening them up to all manner of the cold's attacks. Even those who dread it do so with a certain thrill. For evidence of this, look no further than how it is forecast: as accumulation. How high will it pile, we demand to know. The implication here is one of bounty; the snow, whether we want it or not, is something given to us. All of this obscures what the snow actually does, though, which is that it itself obscures, covers up, takes away.

There is something here, something mournful, but I am too tired to fully understand it. So I take the page with me to my office and add it to all the others.

36.

When we return to the Lookout that morning, the thing in the snow has escaped its most recent dry-erase prison. I move from one side of the room to the other, trying to find an angle at which it could conceivably fit within the circle. Gibbs sits on the floor trying desperately to reconnect two pieces she's certain fit together at the end of yesterday. Cline just stares at the accumulated chair parts.

Despite the previous night's revelations, I feel more confused than ever. I'd camped out in the Lookout. I'd confronted Gilroy in my room. When he told me that it wasn't him—that he wasn't sabotaging our progress—I believed him. But somewhere along the line, my train of thought switched tracks, and I imagined the elimination of my prime suspect would mean these things would stop. But here we are, another week wasted, another task incomplete, and no end in sight.

I don't know how much longer I can go on like this. And I don't know for how long the others will continue without an outright rebellion against me. Unless—and this occurs to me only now—this *is* the rebellion. Gilroy's innocence does not mean there are no potential culprits. It means that before, there were three, and now, there are just two: Gibbs and Cline.

I should take the weekend to plan a surveillance regimen. I should encamp myself in the Lookout all night. I should wait under the cover of darkness until whichever one of them it is—if it's not both of them, working in tandem—happens into the room. And then I should let them know, in no uncertain terms, the extent to which they have underestimated me.

This more measured approach might've been possible had I gotten more sleep, but at present, my reserves of physical and mental energy are depleted, and I find tact entirely out of reach. Before I can stop myself, I turn from the windows and face my colleagues. "Who is it? Who's doing this?"

Cline doesn't even look at me. Gibbs tries once more to find purchase between the pieces she's holding and then sets them down. "What? Doing what?"

"This," I say. "All of this. Someone's coming in here at night. Someone's disconnecting the pieces, and redrawing the circles. Someone's doing it. And it certainly isn't me. So who is it?"

"Why would anyone do that?"

"I don't know," I say. "Perhaps someone might want to drive me to quit so she could assume my position as supervisor."

Gibbs squints at me. "I'm sorry, are you accusing me of something?"

"It would seem that's exactly what I'm doing," I say.

It is a theory I have only just hatched, one that I am not

219

entirely certain of, but saying it aloud still sends a thrill of adrenaline through me, because I've spoken the unspeakable. I've laid out the issue at the root of our tumultuous relationship.

Gibbs doesn't take the bait. "I don't want your job, Hart."

"You asked about opportunities for advancement. Remember?"

"I did?" Gibbs says.

"Yes," I say, definitively, though I can no longer call to mind the exact circumstances of the conversation.

"Okay," Gibbs says. "But that was probably before I realized our job was going to be opening doors all week."

"Oh, so you're too good for this then?" I say. "You're overqualified?"

"Of course I am!" Gibbs says, her voice rising. "Anyone would be overqualified for this job!"

"So why do you stay?" I demand.

"To save some money," Gibbs says. "I might go back to school, I don't know."

"And your decision to torture me by endlessly undermining my authority?" I say. "Was that just to keep yourself entertained?"

"Me? I'm the one torturing you?" Gibbs says. "Do you have any idea how it is to work with you?"

"*For* me," I say.

"Exactly! That's exactly it! You're just so hung up on being some figure of authority," Gibbs says, getting to her feet. "You've got problems, Hart. Real problems."

"No, I have *a* problem, singular," I say, "and I'm looking at her right now."

"Ever notice that there aren't sunsets here?" Cline says.

Gibbs and I turn to him, the non sequitur taking the wind entirely out of our discussion.

Cline doesn't look up from the debris intended to be a chair, piled in the middle of the room. "It just sort of gets dark," he says.

"The cloud cover is dense," I offer.

Cline shakes his head. "I don't think it's the clouds. I've been to cloudy places and they're not like this. For a while, I thought I could figure it out. Here, I mean. I thought this could be something special. I'd get to know the landscape and then I'd use my stipend to have some supplies shipped, and I'd paint it, even with it being so nondescript. Or maybe that was what I thought would be the appeal. Maybe I could make something truly unique, because this place is unique. But I can't solve it. And I thought for a while that it made me a lesser artist. Recently, though, I've been thinking: I don't want to. This place doesn't want to be captured, and I don't want to capture it. I don't want to show it to anyone. I don't want to put anyone through what I go through when I look out the window." Cline blinks hard and rubs his head, as if coming out of a trance. "Sorry, I probably sound crazy."

"It doesn't sound crazy," Gibbs says. She kneels next to Cline and puts a hand on his shoulder. "And it's not a matter of solving it. It can't be solved, because to be solved, it would need to stay the same."

"What are you talking about?" I say.

My tone does not goad Gibbs back into argument. "I'm saying, it's always changing out there."

221

I look out the window, and can see only sameness.

"I noticed it when I was working on the description," Gibbs goes on. "Sometimes, I'd swear the thing in the snow was dark black. The next day, a cobalt blue. The next day, it was rusting. The next day, pristine. I could never pin it down. And it wasn't like I wasn't looking at it. I spent all day staring out there. Sometimes that's all I'd do. I'd look out and blink and it would be dark."

"What do you think it is?" Cline asks.

"I don't know," Gibbs says. "But it's not right. Why doesn't the snow melt? Why doesn't any more snow fall? Why are there no sunsets? Why doesn't it stay where it is? Why don't we ever see it move? Why don't the pieces of the chair stay together? It's like the rules of reality pick and choose when they apply here."

"This is ridiculous," I say.

"Is it?" Gibbs says, and the way she looks at me, it's as if she knows I am coming apart at the seams.

Denial is often born of fear. It grows stronger even as the thing one seeks to deny becomes more and more difficult to dispute. And a sense of denial coupled with exhaustion can breed something else: a dangerous level of brashness. Denying the plainly obvious ceases to be a simple defense mechanism, but instead mutates into a need, one so deep it will spur someone to suggest things they know to be potentially hazardous.

All of this is to explain that, when I propose what I am going to do next, I understand, somewhere deep down, that it's a bad idea.

"Yes," I say, "it is. And I'll prove it."

Cline makes a face like he's just smelled something rancid. "How?"

"By going out there," I say. "And seeing what that thing in the snow is once and for all."

"You're going out there?" Gibbs says.

"Yes," I say, not yet sure I can go through with it.

"I thought that wasn't allowed?" Cline says.

"It's not," I say.

There is a pause during which the others seem engaged in a complicated series of personal calculations, weighing, I'd imagine, the potential risks against the potential excitement of going where we are strictly forbidden to go.

"Can we come?" Cline says.

"If you want," I say.

"We're coming," Gibbs says. And so it is decided.

37.

It takes time for us to gather our outdoor clothes and fetch the buckets from the closet downstairs—my idea, to use as shovels in case the thing in the snow really is just the tip of something much larger. And then it takes more time trying and failing to find a third-story window overlooking the thing in the snow that isn't frozen shut, eventually settling for one facing an entirely different direction that Cline, with some effort, manages to jimmy open. All told, it costs us more than an hour, and in that time the resolve we felt in the Lookout depletes.

Standing next to the open window, feeling the true depth of the cold coming through, Gibbs says, "Are we sure we should do this?" It bothers me that she has already co-opted this mission, turning it from my idea into groupthink, but I know to argue now will doom us.

"It'll be fine," I say, trying my best to hide just how little I believe this. "This is something we need to do."

"What about the snow sickness Kay told us about?" Gibbs says.

"I'm not concerned," I say, another lie. "It's natural to get disoriented in the cold. But we won't be out there long."

"But what if it's not just disorientation?" Cline says, adding in a hoarse whisper: "What if it's the rash?"

"The rash is a birthmark," I say.

Cline cocks his head to one side. "What? Really? Where'd you read that?"

I ignore this. "We ought to get going, before we get too cold just standing here."

Any true confidence that this would all be simple and straightforward lasts only as long as it takes to lower ourselves out of the window. Immediately upon reaching the surface, something feels wrong.

From the highest windows of the Northern Institute, at certain times of day, you can occasionally see that the snow is not smooth but a series of rolling drifts, like crashing waves. I had expected some sense of this on the surface. But no, with the walls of the Institute at our backs, it's not just that the landscape appears flat; what stands in front of us looks two-dimensional, like a blank slate we could reach out and touch. Or, conversely, like there is nothing in front of us at all.

"What side of the building are we on?" I ask.

Gibbs says, "North-facing," just as Cline says, "South." Both sound confident, though I'm fairly certain we are on the west side. I look up, trying to find the sun. The brightest spot I can see in the clouds hangs directly above us, which doesn't exactly compute either: it is at least a few hours to noon. Could I be misinterpreting the angle?

"We should move to higher ground," I suggest. "To get our bearings."

"There's a hill over that way," Cline says. He points at what looks like nothing, but since I don't see anything more promising and neither does Gibbs, we hike in that direction. The snow gives way slightly under us, leaving us ankle deep before our feet meet a layer of compacted ice. It slows our progress, and after walking for nearly ten minutes, it doesn't feel like we've moved at all.

"Should we try another direction?" I ask.

"Why?" Cline asks.

"To find a hill," I say.

"This is a hill," he says. "We're going up. Can't you feel it?"

I shake my head, as does Gibbs, but Cline pays us no attention. He points directly ahead of us. "Wait, is that it?"

Off in the distance, to our left, we can just barely make out the thing in the snow.

"But that doesn't make sense," Gibbs says, "if we came through a north-facing window."

"Or a southern one," Cline says.

Or a western one, I think. My senses are utterly scrambled in every direction. How had I not even realized we were ascending? Why does it feel like the buzzing in my beard has taken on a different, smoother, yet more distracting cadence? Has it channeled deeper somehow? For a moment, dizziness overtakes me. I take a deep breath of cold air and manage to get my footing, the pain in my lungs be damned. This is the longest I've been outside since arriving at the Northern Institute. Any warmth we'd smuggled outside from the heated rooms and hallways is gone now.

Gibbs sighs. "Well, there's only one thing to do." We hike in the direction of the thing in the snow. Within seconds, it seems to duck out of view.

"It's getting away!" Gibbs says.

"We must be going down," I say.

"I can still see it," Cline says, "and I still feel like I'm going up."

I look at him, and he does seem to be on higher ground than Gibbs and me. If it were not for his boots disappearing into the snow, he would appear to be floating. The dizziness returns, and I close my eyes to quell it. Doing so works immediately, which gives me an idea.

"We need to be closer to each other," I say.

Gibbs is on my left and Cline on my right, so I position my bucket between Gibbs and me, and we all link arms.

"Now, we close our eyes," I say.

"What?" Cline says.

"How are we going to see it?" Gibbs asks.

"We'll open our eyes again once we're higher," I say.

The other two agree, half-heartedly, but it works, at least somewhat. Blind and conjoined, we can now feel the topography more acutely. My beard still hums in its newly unpleasant way, but without having to look where I'm going, I'm able to focus my energy on repressing it.

We go up. Then we go down. Then we go up again, before feeling the ground level off, at which point we open our eyes briefly to assess where we are. Again, we see the thing in the snow, but now it's off to our right and looks farther away than before.

Cline, on the right side of our chain, says, "Someone was pulling us to the left."

Gibbs, the sole person who could be accused of the pulling given her position, counters with: "Or someone was too eager, got out in front of the rest of us, and sent us winding in the wrong direction. And I know Hart and I were walking in lockstep, so . . ."

I don't turn from the thing in the snow to look at Cline, but I can tell by the way his arm, interlocked with mine, tenses that the remark hurts him. Just as quickly, something shifts: not a release of the tension, but a change.

"Or," he says, his voice barely above a whisper, "it doesn't want us to reach it."

Now Gibbs's arm goes so stiff that it rattles the bucket between us. She says nothing, but I understand immediately that the idea has snared her too.

I don't like this. Reckless speculation concerning the thing in the snow's power is dangerous enough in the safety of the Northern Institute, but out here, it feels disastrous. We can't give ourselves over to nonsense thoughts like this, not when we're so vulnerable.

"It's not running away. That's preposterous," I say. Am I shouting? "We've just gotten off course."

I try narrowing my eyes, but it does no good. What I see in front of me remains a flat, mostly colorless image with a single disturbance. The feeling in my face battles the bitter cold for dominion of my senses as I try even harder to focus my vision, hoping some recognizable landscape will present itself like an optical illusion. When my dizziness returns with greater strength, I release each of their arms and turn around, looking for some place marker to prove my point.

"Watch it!" Gibbs cries when my bucket bumps her.

I open my mouth to apologize, but can find no words. My throat is full.

I keep turning and the Institute comes into view, not where I expect it and closer than seems reasonable considering how much we've been walking. And that's it. That's all I can take. My knees buckle under me, and the dizziness gives way to full-blown queasiness.

I vomit, staining the snow with bright yellow bile.

38.

The others help me back to the Institute. The walk does not take as long as the walk out, somehow, though it does take us nearly fifteen minutes to locate the window from which we emerged. In the end, we find it around the corner, though, again, none of us can remember rounding a corner when we came out.

Then comes the process of getting me back inside. After Gibbs climbs easily in, I try to pull myself up. The others thankfully attribute my inability to do so to my current state, rather than some failure of upper-body strength. Cline eventually makes a step by cradling his hands, lifting me so that Gibbs can pull me through the open window, a process that results in many strained grunts I am certain will emblazon themselves on my memory, but at least we all make it in safe and sound.

"I'm sorry," I say, once we're inside.

"It's really okay," Gibbs says.

"It must've been something I ate."

Cline and Gibbs exchange a look. "Sure," says Cline.

"Do you need help getting upstairs?" Gibbs asks.

"Oh, I'll be fine," I say, but when I try to move, I find I have some trouble.

"You're sitting," Cline says.

"What?"

"You're sitting," Cline says. "You're on a chair."

I look down. "So I am."

Gibbs moves to my side and gestures for Cline to get the other. Together, they help me to my feet and support me as we slowly proceed all the way up the stairs to the sixth floor, and into my suite. They even bring me to my bed and lay me down.

"Do you need anything?" Gibbs asks. "Some water maybe?"

"No, I'm okay," I tell them, so that I can hear it myself. "I'll be back up in no time."

"I think you should probably stay here for a bit," Gibbs says.

"If you say so, doctor," I say, forcing a laugh.

"Do you want us to, like, work on the chair or the blinds or anything?" Cline asks.

This is when I notice that neither of them appears entirely steady on their feet either. Gibbs sways gently. Cline holds a corner of my desk in a not exactly casual way.

"I don't think that's necessary," I tell them, pulling the blanket up over myself. "Let's regroup and try again next week."

I don't know if they leave before I nod off, or if my nodding off is what spurs them to leave. Whatever the order, that's what happens: they leave, and I nod off. What follows cannot exactly be called sleep. I certainly *approach* sleep, only to experience a falling sensation that jettisons me back to a momentary quasi-wakefulness, at which point the process repeats. This goes on for some time, hardly feeling restful, but when I finally come to—soaked in sweat; I had not taken my outdoor clothes off before getting under the covers—I'm at least somewhat refreshed.

The sun has mostly gone down, meaning it is early in the evening, so I ease myself to the edge of the bed, test my ability to put weight on my legs, and decide to go for a walk, only to arrive in my office a few moments later without any memory of the trip down or of planning this as my destination. When I see the manila folders on the desk, I feel sick with dread. Another week without progress. Another week behind. I sit down and take out the stack of Post-its, but I don't know what to say. I cannot bring myself to write another brief note reassuring Kay that we will get on top of things next week.

I turn to the snow sickness symptom card. It would make perfect sense to fill it out, but I don't want to, and not because I don't want to admit I went out onto the snow, against strict orders. I can't blame a short stint outside for the current state of affairs. We are here because I have failed as a leader, over and over again. I can't pretend I'm capable anymore. I can't pretend things will normalize. So I return the card to its hiding place, take out a notebook, rip out a page, and write:

> *Kay—*
> *I understand the dismay you will experience upon seeing this note where the paperwork should be. Believe me, I feel it tenfold. I'm afraid we may need to have a discussion about my ability to fill the role you have entrusted to me. Since the misunderstanding*

concerning wellness week, we have fallen woefully behind,
and there are no signs we will right the course anytime soon.
As things have gone further and further amiss, I have tried to
delegate responsibility for this failure to anyone but myself. I
thought the others were too distracted. Then I thought someone
was actively sabotaging us. I even went so far as to accuse Gilroy
and Gibbs of this directly. But I realize now that, as a supervi-
sor, I am not allowed the luxury of blaming my colleagues. After
all, our collective failure to stay motivated, to focus and work as
a team, is evidence of my own failure as a leader. And so, while
I would love to ask how you suggest we rectify this situation, I
understand that at this point, having fallen several tasks behind
and been openly antagonistic to a subordinate and a coworker,
the consequences for my lackluster performance may be more se-
vere than some advice.

Best,

Hart

It is painful to write, but after trekking to the roof and depositing it in the lockbox, a sense of relief washes over me. However the note is received, I am happy to have the situation out of my hands.

Back in my quarters, drinking a mug of hot tea, I listen for the helicopter's approach and subsequent retreat, and when it fades into the distance I exhale. Whatever it is that's going to happen will happen in time.

I look around the room. Four bare walls, a desk, a small porthole window. I know that it will take time to hear back from Kay regarding my continued employment status, but still, I can't shake the feeling that this is the end, the last time I'll see this little corner of the Institute that's been my home for the past several months, and I do my best to take it all in.

Which is how my eyes lock on the shelf containing the Leader series, and I suddenly feel entirely ashamed. Writing a letter to put *my* future in someone else's hands? What a weak, cowardly move. So unlike anything Jack French would dream of doing. No, were Jack French to be in this situation, unfathomable as that possibility may be, he certainly would not hang his head and say, "Oh well." He'd do what needed to be done to steady the ship himself. Of course, I cannot call the helicopter back and tear the note to confetti without Kay ever seeing it, but that doesn't mean I have to sit in bed and wait for her to reach out with news of my demotion or dismissal.

I get out of bed and put on my sweater, pants, and boots. Then I return to my office and set the coffee machine to brew. There's work to be done.

39.

Another weekend at the Northern Institute, but only in name.

I load the three remaining task sheets into a single folder, hook a pen to the top of it, and begin.

I start with the blinds. I go from one to the next, carefully standing to the side of each to avoid being consumed by the nothingness of the blind or the gloom of the outside. I pull. I hold. I retract. There are still countless blinds remaining, but I work with swift efficiency. My muscles conform to the task at hand. I learn just how to let go so that the blind remains closed, just how much to tug to send it upward. There are no blinds on the porthole windows of our quarters, so I am able to skip the sixth floor, making my way to the seventh, where there are no blinds either, but the task will not feel done until I have fully ascended the Institute and stand before the wide windows of the amphitheater.

Here, as dawn is just beginning to break on Saturday—something I'm sure of as never before—I cannot help but glance outside. I do my best not to look at the thing in the snow, nor the yellow stain of my vomit (except to note that the two of them appear closer than seems possible, given our experience outside).

The horizon appears more distinct than I've ever seen it, the white of the snow meeting a mean gray sky. But I don't dwell on either of these things. In the blank space on the paperwork where Kay asks for the number of blinds requiring replacement, I proudly write a zero.

Tiles. That is the next task. To examine the tile flooring, with an eye for "wear and tear that may become problematic and result in tripping (dangerous; potential injury) or stumbling (also dangerous: potential injury, by way of hot liquid spilled, for example; demoralizing: potential damage to morale by way of a dropped and subsequently broken keepsake)."

I stare at the sheet for some time. Each task has seemed simple enough at first, only to blindside us with unforeseen volume. Why are there so many chairs, I've wondered, so many tables, so many blinds? They seem to multiply in anticipation of being assessed. But the expanse of tiles underfoot has always seemed endless. So how will their inclusion in the task manipulate my perception of them? Will their endlessness double somehow? Or will the effect be the opposite? Will their actual number pale in comparison to how infinite the tiles *feel*?

Thinking will only prolong things. I lower my head, and I walk, shuffling without picking my feet up off the ground, so that I will perceive any obstruction, running my toe along the edges of each tile to ensure all feels even and flat.

The seventh-floor amphitheater alone takes what feels like several hours. On the sixth floor, I walk quietly, checking the hallways and all of the rooms except those occupied by Cline and Gibbs, making a note to ask them about their tiles when next I see them. Eventually, I make it to the fifth floor. When I get tired I lie down where I am, resting my head on the last tile I checked, and briefly sleep.

Progress is gradual. Two things slow me down. The first is my beard.

I no longer feel nauseous from the trip out onto the snow, but my beard still throbs as it did when we were outside, making my face feel unpleasantly warm and tense. Several times, I catch myself staring up at the light fixture of a room, trying in vain to interpret the synchronicity of its buzz with the agitation in my face, and, having lost track of my examination of the tiles, I have to start the entire room all over again.

Finally, I make a difficult decision. I write the number of the fifth-floor room I'm in on my hand, and then I set out for my quarters, retrieve a pair of scissors and my razor, go to the suite bathroom, and shave.

Looking in the mirror, I am surprised to see myself like this, and not just because of my undefined chin. I appear feminine in a way that I can't quite place, as if I am my own sister visiting for the weekend. But it works. Now that I am smooth-faced for the first time in years, the hum retreats. I feel fresh, rejuvenated.

Absentmindedly, I wash my hands before leaving the bathroom, wiping away the number. I don't expect this to be a problem, assuming that I'll be able to find where I left off anyway, but when I resume my work, all the rooms are anonymous. I start over from the beginning of the fifth floor.

The other thing that slows me down is Gilroy, who first appears in the midmorning. Gilroy has had no problem making himself scarce for almost the entirety of my time at the Northern Institute, but suddenly, I can't avoid him. He crosses my path in the hallway often, and will darken the doorway of whichever room I'm in.

His sole purpose for interrupting me is to report on the developing weather. "It's snowing," he says, casually at first, but after several occasions when I don't respond—don't even raise my eyes from the floor, in fact—he begins simply shouting, "Snow!" When he does this I can't help but jump and look up from the tiles to find him gesturing madly toward the window. "Snow!" he'll repeat. "Snow!" before retreating to some shadowy corner of the building, leaving me disoriented and no longer sure of my progress or direction.

Finally, when I've nearly finished examining the tiles of the third floor, he appears again, once more shouting, "Snow!" This time, he manages to slip past me into the room I currently occupy and stands directly in front of the window. Behind him, snow is indeed falling, but it's hard to tell how hard. The flakes, against the backdrop of the gray horizon and the expanse of already frozen snow, register as little more than a static-like sparkle. Still, I say to Gilroy, "Yes, it is."

This, apparently, is all he was after. He nods and walks hastily out of the room. I do not see him again.

I keep going, napping when I need to, with my head on the last tile I've inspected. Despite this sporadic rest schedule (the absence of a schedule, really) and the lack of natural light (I'm making swift progress through the second floor) I remain mostly anchored in terms of time and day. But without Gilroy's visits, my mind returns to the task at hand before eventually starting to wander.

To avoid thinking about Kay receiving my message, I occupy myself with a fantasy of Monday morning: Cline and Gibbs arriving at the office, their shoulders slumped, their faces filled with dread, until I proclaim the seemingly insurmountable pile of tasks that has accumulated over the past few weeks to be no more. I have taken it upon myself to complete the outstanding work. I play out this scene over and over again, and in one instance, they even come to realize what a gift it is to be given an hour for coffee and light socialization each morning, and express as much with great sincerity.

As I move on to the first floor, however, the fantasy breaks down. My miraculous completion of the tasks would likely involve a discussion about my recovery following our journey onto the snow. They did agree to join me on said journey, but I was the catalyst. This reframes the narrative. No longer can I see myself as heroic. Quite the contrary, the entire undertaking would seem a tacit admission of my wrongdoing as a leader. One that would be made less than tacit by whatever disciplinary action Kay decides to take in response to the message, which, again, I try not to think about. And as I am actively trying not to think about this very thing—and in so doing, thinking about it—I stare at a tile and something strikes like a lightning bolt: this is the last one. I take the sheet from the folder and fill a zero in where it asks for the number of tiles that require replacing.

I choose to forgo the chair for now. I've got real momentum and I don't want to get waylaid. The only remaining task is to open all the windows and test their mechanisms. To thaw those that are frozen shut, Kay has provided the hair dryer.

At the bottom of the paperwork, I find an additional note: "For this task, employees are required to don their outdoor gear, as the process will become quite cold. Frequent breaks are recommended. The task only applies to windows above the snow line. Windows below the snow line must remain closed at all times. Upon completion of this task, employees will receive a small bonus to compensate for the minor health risks associated with continued exposure to the cold air."

Only, the risk is not so minor now. Outside, the static of the flakes has ramped up. The snowstorm has mutated into a full-blown blizzard.

Considering that the portholes in our rooms do not open, I retrieve the hair dryer from my office and my outdoor gear from my quarters and begin work on the fifth floor. It is here that time starts to elude me.

Moving through the building, I run the hair dryer around the edges of each window until I can feel some give, and then it is not unlike when you know you're carrying a static charge and yet must put your hand on a metal doorknob. The coming unpleasantness causes you to pause, but the pause only delays the inevitable. The difference is, in opening the windows to the blizzard, it is not just a mild shock but a sensation more like momentary drowning. The cold air and icy snow rushes me, finding any opening. My nostrils go numb. My eyes water. I dare not open my mouth lest I risk being choked.

At first, the effect is one of days passing. Each time I open a window is like nightfall, each time I close it, like morning. The in-between, in which the blizzard briefly tries to strangle me, is the most terrible kind of sleep. Over time it only gets worse, so that it feels less like a series of tiny days punctuated by the bursts of cold and snow than like miniature lifetimes, each opening a death, each closing a birth.

It occurs to me, in a brief moment of lucidity as I travel from one room to the next, that I am approaching something dangerously close to madness. I look for a way to steady myself. I think of what inspired me to do this in the first place, the Leader series. Those books have kept me anchored in some of my densest weekend fogs. Perhaps they could help now.

Returning to my quarters, taking the hair dryer with me (it does not occur to me that I could leave it, thus providing myself with a marker of where I left off), I gather all the books in my arms, those I have read and those I haven't, unsure what would be most beneficial to my sanity: something new and thrilling, or something comforting and familiar.

It turns out not to matter. I cannot tell the difference between them. I run the hair dryer, I open a window, I die, I close the window, I am reborn. Then, I open a book, and it seems both distant and familiar. There is a collapsed aqueduct and a stranded team of entomologists who disagree about wing classifications. There is an accident in an abandoned mine and a group of mean-spirited pastors. There is a remote, rentable tree house, a fugitive on the loose, and several park rangers with low self-esteem. There is a coastal bed-and-breakfast and some problematically competitive shell collectors. All of them call something to mind, but when I try to play out the plot in my head, I can't tell whether I'm remembering, or grafting the characters onto the story from another one.

Then, finally, I reach one that is undeniably new: *Hot Lava*.

There is no mention of Jack French's ne'er-to-be-completed treatise on management. Instead, the book opens with a briefing from some high-up government official. The private jet of a professional bikini volleyball team has been hijacked by members of a criminal organization who have flown it back to a small tropical island, the defining feature of which is a volcano whose rock face looks like the skull of a buffalo. The volleyball players are being held in a special prison built into the inside of said volcano, and the high-ranking government official can think of just one man for the job: Jack French. Jack French agrees, of course, and over the next two hundred pages displays none of the cunning or sly cleverness that has defined him throughout the series. The only mention of leadership at all occurs when Jack French notes the homographic quality of the words "lead," the verb on which he has made a name for himself, and "lead," the material from which munitions are forged, before opening fire with a machine gun while zip-lining over a pit of lava. It is an overwritten and clunky piece of wordplay the first time it occurs; the three subsequent times the exact same joke is deployed are only worse. Its final repetition comes in the climax, during a duel with the criminal organization's leader, who is, for some reason, the sole guard of the aforementioned interior volcano prison. Jack French dispatches the masked man quickly, and I expect some twist, given that nearly a quarter of the book remains, but no. What follows is an argument between the members of the bikini volleyball team in terms of who might be given the privilege of thanking Jack French before determining they can all thank him together in a way that seems entirely inappropriate and unprofessional for Jack French to accept. This act of thanks—which, despite its level of detail, involves a number of anatomical improbabilities— occupies the remainder of the pages.

Skimming the final several chapters, I'm confused that Rodney Stuyvesant Jr. would take the series in this bizarre direction, but as I close the book, I notice something that I had overlooked at the outset. The author on the front is no longer listed as Rodney Stuyvesant Jr.; it's Rod Stuyvesant III. In the back, I find his bio.

ROD STUYVESANT III, part-time professional wind surfer and author of the internationally bestselling Leader series, likes his character development like he likes his mai tais: strong!

That this is where things were ultimately leading taints them all. I drop the books out of the next window I hair-dry open. The accumulating snow quickly engulfs them.

I am not sure how much time has passed. It seems like years since I last saw daylight. When I go to the bathroom, I avoid the mirror, fearful that I will see gray hair, a long beard, sunken cheeks. I am on the fourth floor, but have I completed my check of the windows here? Or have I gone around twice? Five times? A thousand times? However many times it's been, it's enough. I find the door to the stairwell and make my way down.

I have not seen the others this whole time, and I grow convinced that they've left, quit, abandoned me without notice—and after the danger I put them in with our trip out onto the snow, who could blame them? Then again, it seems impossible that they'd be able to leave in this blizzard, which still rages on, all these lifetimes later. This is the contradiction I try to parse on my way down, en route to the third floor, but in my current cold-addled state, the only conclusion I can find is that they didn't leave because they were never really here. They never existed. I've always been alone here at the Northern Institute. Perhaps that explains my recent failures of memory, in terms of the concrete details from before the thing in the snow's arrival: it's difficult to recall what never really happened.

In a panic, I rush through the first rooms across from the door to the stairwell, trying to picture either of them, Gibbs or Cline, when I close my eyes to the harsh burst of the cold. Then, in my office, I see the Post-its left on the desk, and they are like a life raft to my shipwrecked mind. I can preserve reality, whether it is real or not. All I need to do is write it.

I take the Post-its with me. The entire process—the hair dryer, the window, the cold—becomes a blur. All of my energy is focused on getting the words down. After one window, I write:

I thought she wanted my job, but really she was just saving money.

After the next, I write another:

He's a painter, but we've never seen him paint.

After the next, another:

She comes from a place where the wind is so strong, it can blow out a candle through a closed window, so to speak.

And another:

He asked me to describe a lamp without using the word "lamp."

And another:

She selected the rooms where we would meet, and I allowed it.

And another:

He has seen still life paintings so subversive, he cannot give voice to their contents.

And another:

She is destined for greater things than me.

And another:

I thought he was the hiker, but he is the rash.

And another:

It is just a birthmark, not a rash, despite what the tables say.

And another:

It appears soft like a pillow, yet hard as stone.

And another:

It seems to expand as it goes up but comes to a narrow tip that is both sharp and blunt all at once.

And another:

It shines in a subdued way that is glossy and also matte.

And another:

I open a window. I die.

And another:

I close a window. I am reborn.

And another:

I open a window. I die.

And another:

I close a window. I am reborn.

And another:

I open a window. I die.

And another:

I close a window. I am reborn.

I stick these notes to any flat surface I see: the windowsills, tables, desks, in some cases the floor. When the Post-its run out, I go looking for more.

In this way, an eternity at the Northern Institute passes.

40.

I wake to a distant shout and am greeted by a complex network of text: words scrawled in neat blocks, some right side up, some upside down, some going this way, some that. Altogether it forms an asymmetrical plaid, but what is it all? Might this be the frame through which all of the world is filtered for me from now on? Has my failure to find more Post-its resulted in my unreleased thoughts accumulating inkily over my vision?

The shout comes again, a call, my name: "Hart?"

"I'm here!" I call back. I try to sit up but bang my head against the underside of the table. How I got here, I don't exactly know. I roll out and get to my feet, my legs stiff and my back sore from sleeping on cold tile for who knows how long.

"There you are!" Gibbs says, appearing in the doorway. Her expression goes from relief to shock, but she composes herself quickly. "You shaved."

"Yes, I did." I run my hand over my face, rough with a dusting of stubble. Impossible. How is the growth not more substantial than this? "What day is it?"

Gibbs looks around the room as if searching for some cause of my disorientation. "Monday," she says.

"But how many Mondays has it been?" I ask.

"How many Mondays?" Gibbs repeats.

"Since we last saw each other," I say.

"Since Friday?" Gibbs says. "Zero Mondays?"

So it was only a weekend, I think. One eternal weekend. "And now it's Monday afternoon?"

"It's about ten in the morning, I think," Gibbs says. "We waited until about nine thirty, and when you didn't show we got worried, you know, especially after what happened out on the snow, and then the whole thing with Gilroy—" She stops abruptly and looks me up and down. "Wait, why are you in your outdoor clothes? Did you try and go out there again?"

At her acknowledgment of my attire, sweat blooms in my armpits. "I didn't go outside, no. I mean, I had some exposure to the storm. But nothing that the work didn't call for."

"The work?" Once again, she looks around the room, and this time her eyes find the hair dryer on the floor. "What work?"

"Just our tasks," I say. "I worked through the weekend to get them done."

"All of them?" Gibbs says.

"Yes," I say, and I can't help but feel a bit of pride, which Gibbs unknowingly stamps out immediately.

"You figured out the chair?" she says.

"All of the tasks but the chair."

Gibbs cannot hide her disappointment. "Oh."

Just thinking about the chair brings back the tension at the end of last week, and I realize what I need to do. I take a deep breath. "Gibbs, I'm sorry. About last Friday."

"We agreed to go with you," Gibbs says. "That's on us."

"I mean before that, in the Lookout," I clarify. "I said some things, and they weren't kind. And I'm sorry."

Gibbs blinks. I can't tell if the look on her face is one of surprise or suspicion, both warranted, I guess. She opens her mouth to respond, but hesitates, which is when we hear the sound of the stairwell door opening down the hall.

"Hey, we got helicopters," Cline calls out.

We meet him in the hallway and he says, "Oh good. You're okay," before doing a double take. "Cheeks," is all he can stammer.

I raise my hand to my face automatically.

Cline interprets this as self-consciousness. "No, it's great. Cheeks are great. I mean, I like it. You look good."

"Thank you," I say.

"Did you say the helicopter is here?" Gibbs says.

"And you're sure it's Monday," I say to Gibbs.

"It's definitely Monday," Gibbs says, her concern already fading to frustration with my continued insistence that more time has passed.

"No, not *the* helicopter," Cline says. "Helicopters. Like, plural."

41.

We rush upstairs. At the sixth-floor landing, we meet a group of seven men and women, all wearing matching jackets. The logo stitched onto the breast of each one seems vaguely familiar, and with some effort, I'm able to recall it printed atop the contract I signed when I took this position.

A woman holding a cardboard box steps forward from behind a bald man with piercing eyes. Barely five feet tall and of compact build, Kay nevertheless carves an intimidating figure. What she lacks in stature, she makes up for with an unflinchingly stern countenance, betraying so little emotion, positive or negative, it is impossible not to assume she is thinking the worst of you at any given moment.

This is how I feel as she looks from one of us to the next.

"I received your message," she says. "I apologize for not coming sooner, but the weather posed some difficulties. It still does, actually. The helipads need shoveling, for one. But that can be dealt with in time. Right now I need you to tell me: Where is he?"

I had no idea my cry for help would be met so quickly and with such intensity, but so be it. Better to get it out of the way. I step forward from the other two. "I'm right here, Kay. It's me. I've just shaved my characteristic beard is all."

"Gilroy," Kay says. "Where is Gilroy?"

The question surprises me, not just because it isn't what I was expecting, but because Gilroy is not a member of my team, so I have no idea why I'd be expected to know his whereabouts. Which is why it is equally surprising when Cline answers, "He's in my room."

Moments later, standing in the doorway to his quarters, looking at Gilroy where he rests in Cline's bed, appearing pale but comfortable, Cline explains in a hushed voice what happened: At some point during the weekend, he'd left his suite to exercise in the stairwell, but was shocked by how cold it was. He made his way up to the roof to investigate and found that someone had opened the door, which then got stuck in the accumulation of snow. As he worked to shut it, he noticed a small snowy mound about twenty feet from the door. He assumed it to be nothing more than a snowdrift.

Only when he noticed the faint indents of footprints, rapidly filling in and barely visible, did it occur to him to check the mound, which he did, despite wearing just his exercise clothes. It was Gilroy. Cline managed to get him over his shoulder and brought him back here, found Gibbs, and the two of them had spent the weekend watching him, getting him to drink some tea when he was able.

"But only herbal tea," Cline says. "Nothing caffeinated, because he needed his rest."

"Very good," Kay says. She turns to one of the men gathered in the suite hallway. "There are emergency blankets in the helicopters. Gather some of those and bundle him up for the journey home."

It takes only a few minutes for the man to disappear and return, and only another few for three of them to wrap Gilroy, who barely rouses, and take him with them. When he's gone Kay turns to the three of us, her eyes focusing on me. "I take it by the casual nature with which you mentioned him in your letter that you did not realize Gilroy should not be here."

"No, I didn't realize," I say, though perhaps somewhere deep down, I did.

"And that he received no communication," Kay says, "nor an official allotment of provisions, this did not raise any red flags?"

"So wait, Gilroy was the provisions thief?" Cline whispers to Gibbs, in reference to something I've never heard them discuss. I try not to speculate on who they originally hypothesized to be the "provisions thief."

"I guess I just imagined he had his work, and that he retrieved his provisions before I unloaded ours," I say. "I'm sorry. You're right. This was an oversight on my part."

"You must not apologize. This is an issue of our making." Kay's remaining cronies stand behind her in the suite hallway, an unblinking wall of authority. But when she says this, she looks back to them, and they all avert their eyes. She turns once

254

again to us. "We have put you in potential danger, housing you here in this facility with a very unstable individual."

"Danger?" says Gibbs.

"Very unstable?" says Cline.

"I can explain everything," Kay says.

"Everything?" I say. "Really? Everything?"

"Yes," Kay says. "It will take a moment, if you would prefer to get comfortable."

We move into Cline's room, he and Gibbs sitting on his bed and me at the desk chair. Kay and her team remain standing.

"Gilroy was a researcher here," Kay says, "when the facility was fully operational. He was not what you might call popular. But he was especially close with one of the others."

"Donnelly," I say. "His friend."

Kay turns to me. "Yes. Donnelly. And 'friend' is a word one might use."

"They weren't friends?" I say.

Kay stares at me without speaking.

"They were more than friends?" I say.

"It would be unprofessional of me to comment further," Kay says. "The important thing to understand is that they were close. What else is important is that Donnelly, for his part, was popular among the other researchers. This stemmed from his seeming immunity to the snow sickness you have all been briefed on, an immunity he flaunted by taking long walks around the Institute."

"So Donnelly is the hiker," Gibbs says.

"But who had the rash?" Cline asks.

"I told you. The rash is a birthmark," I say.

One of Kay's people lets out a small noise that might be a stifled cough but sounds more like a snort.

"I fear we have gone off topic," Kay says. "Yes, Donnelly was often referred to as 'the hiker' here at the Northern Institute. And this was ultimately what spelled his end. The others goaded him to go farther and farther, and eventually, he decided he would attempt to camp upon its surface. He had not been out there more than two hours, though, when a snowstorm came upon us. Donnelly was lost, and the board decided to discontinue the project's funding, fearing litigation. This all happened very quickly. The rushed process of loading and removing the research equipment took the most effort, leaving little time for an orderly evacuation. Head counts were rushed and Gilroy was able to slip through. How he survived the intervening weeks between our departure and your arrival, I cannot be sure, except to say that, around here, you build a certain resilience to inhumane conditions."

Her team nods solemnly at this.

"We probably would have found him if we had returned for the full clear-out, as originally planned," Kay says.

"'The full clear-out'?" Gibbs says. "You mean, what? The rest of the furniture?"

"Yes," Kay says.

"So we wouldn't have had any tables or chairs or anything?" Cline says, before something dire occurs to him and his eyes go wide. "You would've left the beds, right? We'd need something to sleep on. The potential back damage of lying on the floor every night would be platinum-level."

Kay is quiet a moment. Her expression conveys nothing, but I imagine she must be considering what to say next, as she is not someone who would allow for unnecessary silences. "In the interest of full transparency," she says at last, "the initial plan did not call for a caretaking team. This was something we decided on between the evacuation and the proposed date of the clear-out. Our investors were disappointed by rumors of the abandonment. Yes, to continue researching after Donnelly's loss would certainly be problematic, but to so hastily discontinue a project did not inspire confidence in our abilities. We needed a compromise, a way to maintain the building as a non-abandoned structure that is only presently devoid of research. This decision is what resulted in your installation here."

"I thought we were here to keep things in order," Gibbs says, "in case the researchers come back."

"Correct," Kay says. "That is how we framed things at your hiring, and that is how we will continue to frame the situation when discussing it with our investors. In the eyes of our insurers, this is an experimental living cooperative and storage facility."

For my part, I am struggling to put the pieces together. "So, it was a campsite?" I turn to Cline. "Just like you said, when we were testing the tables."

"Wait, I said what now?" Cline says.

"There was no campsite," Kay says. "By all accounts, Donnelly was still hiking toward the horizon when the snowstorm came."

"But it's not a body," I say. "We're sure of that."

"I do not follow," Kay says.

"You said you'd explain everything," I say, and I can hear myself growing agitated, but I don't care. "But I'm telling you, it's not a body. So what is it?"

"What is what?" Kay says.

"What else?" I say. "The thing in the snow."

42.

I insist that we go to the Lookout for the best view. Not even the wall of glass in the amphitheater provides quite so perfect a framing.

Upon our arrival, we are greeted by a mess of chair parts, and a jolt of embarrassment goes through me. We'd always made a point of ordering them—or attempting to, at any rate—but we didn't return to clean up after our expedition onto the snow, and in the trancelike state of the working weekend, I must've wandered straight past them.

"What has happened here?" Kay asks.

Cline and Gibbs look at the ceiling and the floor, respectively.

"There was some difficulty," I say, "with the chair you sent. The labels came off the pieces. And we didn't understand the language of the instructions."

Kay makes a noise like clearing her throat that I only realize is a name when the bald man with the piercing eyes steps forward, saying, "Yes?"

"Did you purchase this chair?" Kay asks.

The man smiles proudly and speaks with an accent I cannot place. "Yes. And for a very favorable price."

"They cannot understand it." Kay motions to the pieces. "Please, assemble."

Without a word, the man goes to work, gathering the instructions where we'd left them in the corner.

"You must excuse the mistake," Kay tells us. "We have an international workforce. This allows us few barriers in our dealings. We are able to easily communicate with and source materials from a wider range of suppliers than most organizations."

"Interesting," I say.

"Where shall I deposit?" the man asks. He stands beside a fully assembled chair. Kay looks to me.

"The seventh floor," I say. "On the stage."

The man's expression transforms from satisfaction to confusion. Even the other two members of Kay's team, a man and a woman who linger behind her in the doorway, turn their attention to me. Cline and Gibbs, realizing a shift in the energy, retreat further into themselves.

"This chair is made of plastic and aluminum," Kay says. "The chair on the stage is the lecturer's chair. It must be wooden. Such is the expectation in our circles."

"I'm sorry," I say. "I didn't realize."

"Disassemble it," Kay says to the man. "And take it to the helicopter. We can get a refund. As for the lecturer's chair, it is not of concern. There will be no lectures here for the foreseeable future."

The man makes a silent show of his frustration, but he takes the chair apart as quickly as he put it together, packing the pieces neatly into the box. The other two move into the room to make way for him. One of them, the man, steps to a table and picks up a Post-it, showing it to the other.

I hear him say, in a hushed tone, "'I close a window. I am reborn.' Was this him, you think?"

"Has to be, right?" the woman whispers.

"It's like whatever was on his back spread to his brain," the man replies.

If Kay hears them, she makes no indication. "Now, where is this object you all seem so taken by?"

"You can see it right out there," I tell her, and I point to the window before looking myself and finding a web of connected circles, each of them containing nothing but brilliant white, freshly fallen snow.

Gibbs and Cline look now, as well.

"It's gone," Gibbs says.

"It got away," Cline says.

"It was covered up by the blizzard," I say.

"I can provide a whiteboard, if you would like to—" But Kay, unable to discern the meaning of the circles, lets the sentence hang there a moment, unfinished, before moving on. "It would be more comfortable, as the window can be quite cold."

"There was something out there," Cline says.

"It is out there," I say. "Under the snow."

"The thing I wrote about," Gibbs says.

"What room is this?" Kay asks, looking around.

"The Lookout," Cline says. Kay raises her eyebrows.

I again feel a surge of embarrassment. "We have names for some of the rooms. And we call this one 'the Lookout.'"

"Because it has more windows than the average room," Kay says. "Clever."

"Yes, exactly!" I say much too loudly, looking across the windows. She's right: there are five of them, whereas most rooms have two or three. That must be why we called it "the Lookout" in the first place.

"But I need the room number," Kay says.

One of her employees, the woman, steps to the door and reads it to her.

"Hmm. No. There would be nothing of concern," Kay says. "Not out this way. Now, you mentioned something about outstanding tasks in your message—"

"They're all complete now," I tell her. Then, I realize something. "I just need to find the paperwork, if you'll give me a minute to look."

"It is not of importance," Kay says. "Just deposit it at the end of the week. What I was going to say was, do not become too concerned with the assignments. They are really for your own good, to keep you occupied. Per what we discussed earlier, your presence alone here is enough for us to keep the lights on, in a manner of speaking, which is the ultimate goal."

"Huh," I say.

"With that being said, as I mentioned before, you have been put in some danger, and so you will all be getting raises," Kay tells us.

"Nice," Cline says.

"I have spoken to the board," Kay goes on. "And they have agreed to grant these raises in either monetary compensation or degrees of temperature here at the Northern Institute."

I turn to Gibbs. "You said you were trying to save some money."

Gibbs shakes her head. "I barely spend anything here."

"Do the degrees," Cline says.

"We'll take the raise in degrees," I tell Kay.

"Very good," Kay says. Then, she holds out the small box she's been carrying this whole time. "Oh, I nearly forgot. It is not generally our policy to encourage frivolity, but it seemed strange that we would come here today, of all days, and not bring something."

I take the box and open the lid, finding a small chocolate cake inside. "Is this," I say, "for telling you about Gilroy?"

"It is for your birthday," Kay says. "It is your birthday today, is it not? Otherwise there may be a paperwork error that requires correcting."

I don't know how to respond to this. The swirling mix of confusion and excitement leaves me light-headed. Really, what could I have expected? That I could entirely lose track of the day, month, and year and still easily locate the date of my birth in the haze?

"Yes," I say because I need to say something. Then: "Of course. It's my birthday. I just didn't expect such a courtesy. Thank you."

"Certainly," Kay says. "Now, we must be going. It is a long flight back to headquarters."

"Can we walk you to the roof?" Gibbs offers.

But Kay shakes her head. "No," she says. "Because I will be stopping at the thermostat."

And with that, she and her employees turn to leave, a less huffy version of the exit I'd grown so used to with Gilroy.

"Wait, one last thing," Cline says. Kay stops in the doorway and turns. "What did you all study at this place?"

"This place," Kay says.

"Oh, sorry," Cline says. "What did you all study here at, what's it called again? The Northern Institute?"

"No," Kay says. "I was answering you. At this place, we studied this place. This region is unique. Perhaps you have noticed."

No one knows how to respond to this, so it is quiet for a moment. Finally, Cline speaks up.

"I don't know," he says. "Seems fine to me."

43.

After all the excitement of the morning, the three of us unload the week's provisions but decide to leave the week's task in the lockbox for the day. Instead, we go to my office, put on a pot of coffee, and cut the cake. I sit behind my desk and the others assume a familiar formation—Cline across from me, Gibbs at the end table with the coffee machine—and a small, impromptu birthday celebration follows, during which we mostly recount the events of the past seventy-two hours. We finish the coffee, but there's still cake left.

"Should we make another pot?" Gibbs asks.

"How about something stronger than coffee?" I suggest.

I excuse myself a moment, climb up to my quarters, and return with a fresh bottle of fortified wine. It's still early, but Gibbs and Cline do not object. Gibbs seems to intuit its value and potency and pours herself only a little bit. Cline fills his mug to the brim.

"Whoa," he says, taking a large drink. "This is like wine but good."

We continue to talk, mostly about how pleasant it feels inside being a few degrees warmer and whether or not this feeling will fade over time, until Cline changes the subject. "Anyone else feel like it was weird what she said? When we tried to show her the thing in the snow?"

"She said that there's nothing to be concerned about." There's an edge to Gibbs's voice, a desire for this remark of hers to convey some finality. This much is clear to me, but Cline, mildly intoxicated, does not pick up on it.

"No," Cline says, "she said there is nothing of concern *out that way.*"

"Okay," Gibbs says. "We don't need to argue semantics."

"It just kind of makes you wonder, doesn't it?" Cline taps his temple with his now-empty mug.

"Cline," Gibbs says.

"Like what there might be——" Cline begins to say.

"Cline!" Gibbs gestures to me. "We're celebrating Hart's birthday."

The bluntness of this finally gets through to him. Cline hangs his head. "Sorry. You're right."

"You were going to say, what there might be in some of the other directions," I say, putting my mug down on the desk.

Cline looks at me apologetically. "I was just riffing," he says.

"I was actually curious," I say, "to get your takes on something else Kay said. About how the tasks——"

"That they don't matter?" Gibbs says. "Because we're really just here as an excuse to keep the power running?"

"That was weird," Cline adds.

266

"It was," I agree. "But I've been thinking about it as we've been sitting here, and I choose not to see it as demeaning. Rather, I think this could be an opportunity for us."

"An opportunity?" Gibbs says.

"Following the events of the morning, as well as last Friday," I tell them, "I have, as the supervisor of this small team, made an executive decision. The tasks worked for us up to a point, but I've seen and experienced a significant dip in morale that leads me to believe they're no longer serving the purpose Kay laid out, of keeping us occupied, or, indeed, sane."

"So the executive decision is no more work?" Cline says.

"Not exactly," I clarify. "We will continue to do the tasks; abandoning them altogether might arouse concern for our mental well-being, and also draw more attention to the fruitlessness of our being here. But we will do them quickly, without as much concern or attention to detail. That will give us time to focus on something more engaging, something that has demanded our attention for some time, and I imagine will continue to demand our attention even now, after it has disappeared."

"The thing in the snow," Gibbs says.

"Exactly." I have not had as much of the fortified wine as Cline. Still, I can feel its effects, which is why I decide to make such a grand gesture: I stand from my desk and motion for Gibbs to take my place.

"You want to trade seats?" she says.

"You've studied it closer than anyone," I say. "I want you to tell us about it."

Gibbs rolls her eyes as we switch places, as if made sheepish by the theatricality of it all, before sitting with a rigid, authoritative posture that betrays her pride. "So, what do you want to know?"

"Let's start," I say, "with everything."

ACKNOWLEDGMENTS

A huge thanks to: my editor, Nate Lanman, and my agent, Kent Wolf, for believing in the weird little project that is this book; my mom, my dad, Brian, and Seamus, for believing in the weird not-so-little person that is me; my first readers, Frank McGinnis, Alex Madison, Keith Eyrich, and Kris Bartkus, for their insight and encouragement; Chandler and Penny, for being such terrible cats and such great companions; Emma, for just, like, everything; and Muriel, who made me a father and, in turn, taught me to be a better man.

ABOUT THE AUTHOR

Sean Adams lives in Des Moines, Iowa, with his wife, Emma, and daughter, Muriel. His first novel, *The Heap*, was a *New York Times* Editors' Choice and was listed among the best books of 2020 by NPR. His stories have been published in *The Magazine of Fantasy & Science Fiction*, Electric Literature's Recommended Reading, and elsewhere.